FUTURE

An unknown avenger... 21st-century Texas. He i... to survive. No public enemy is safe from his instant justice.

Gangland's top enforcer heads the search for the stranger, unaware that his own murderous past holds the secret to the mystery. Many must die before the truth is known at the final showdown . . .

THE LAST RANGERS

"One riot, one Ranger."—Motto of the legendary Texas Rangers, world's best crimefighters. But now it's A.D. 2035—a savage world of battle machines, beam weapons, and high-tech avengers.

Hidden in a cave is the secret base of the last Rangers. For years they've been gathering their powers for the coming struggle. Alamo Smith, champion of lost causes, is the first of their new breed of peacekeepers: a cyber-crusader—a one-man riot squad on a hellbent quest for justice.

THE LAST RANGERS

JAKE DAVIS

BERKLEY BOOKS, NEW YORK

THE LAST RANGERS

A Berkley Book/published by arrangement with
the author

PRINTING HISTORY
Berkley edition / August 1992

ISBN: 0-425-13299-4

A BERKLEY BOOK® TM 757,375
Berkley Books are published by The Berkley Publishing Group,
200 Madison Avenue, New York, New York 10016.
The name "Berkley" and the "B" logo
are trademarks belonging to Berkley Publishing Corporation.

PRINTED IN THE UNITED STATES OF AMERICA

10 9 8 7 6 5 4 3 2 1

"One riot, one Ranger."

—Motto of the Texas Rangers

"Texas—the last best hope of the USA."

—J. D.

ONE

A SKY-HIGH SENTINEL stood watch over Texas. Neither spirit nor flesh, the sentry was a machine made of lightweight high-tensile metalloys, ceramics, racked scaffolds of gridded laser holography crystals, and miles worth of micro-etched printed circuitry. It was crammed with telemetric and communications hardware.

It was *Lone Star Sat*, an eye-in-the-sky spy satellite that floated in geo-synchronous orbit twenty-three thousand miles above the Texas plains. It looked down on an uneasy world wracked by catastrophes both natural and man-made. A hole as big as Ohio gaped in the ozone layer above the South Pole; a smaller hole, Rhode Island–sized, punctured the ozone over the Arctic Circle. Melting polar ice caps had raised the sea level, swamping many of the world's great coastal cities. Turbulence beneath the earth's crust had created new belts of live volcanos, submerged some island chains, and upthrust new ones from the sea bottoms. The recent North Pacific Mega-quake, the long-dreaded Big One, had erased a third of the old California coastline.

The greatest catastrophe of all, though, was the population explosion. People continued to outbreed the planet's capacity to feed them all. The result: a neverending chaos of famine, crime, plague, and war.

Such was the state of the world in the year A.D. 2035.

Lone Star Sat kept on the lookout for dangers that might threaten the great state that had birthed it and lofted it into space. It was the far-seeing and far-hearing eyes and ears of Texas. Arrayed banks of eagle-eyed reconnaissance cameras and electromagnetic signal wave detectors monitored a land mass the size of France. It tracked killer storms in the Gulf, volcanic eruptions in the Vulcan Belt along the Border, cyclonic activity in the Panhandle, tremors in the Ozark earthquake zone.

It also guarded against the potential violence of those who hated Texas, enemies both foreign and domestic who sought to conquer or destroy her. Texas was big, strong, rich, and independent. Her wealth was envied and her maverick ways hated by persons who had less and wanted more and preferred stealing to working for it. The satellite's neutrino spy rays probed the ocean depths for enemy submarines and undersea bases. Its No-Sparrow-Falls space-borne radar net detected unidentified aircraft while they were still well outside striking range; ground-based surface-to-air SAM missile batteries swiftly destroyed them if they persisted in remaining unidentified. Infrared sensors, sensitive enough to detect a match flame flickering on the ground, searched ceaselessly for the telltale heat signature from the exhaust of a hostile missile being launched. Surveillance cameras eyed the movements of navies in the Gulf and armies in Mexico and Central America.

There were other, subtler threats, which the satellite could not see: the schemes of the greedy, the violence of the lawless, the murderousness of ruthless adventurers. A band of farsighted individuals had foreseen the dangers, though, and planned accordingly. They had found a champion, armed and armored him as no man had ever been armed and armored before, and sent him on a mission to bring law and order to the wild world of Texas, A.D. 2035.

This is his story.

TWO

A CAGEFUL OF crooks settled to the ground in front of the county sheriff's substation in Beamer Junction shortly after sunrise. Beamer Junction was a way station midway between San Antonio, Texas, and Del Rio on the Border. The substation was an igloo-shaped concrete bunker that was buried underground except for its dome-shaped top, a hump that protruded above the surface like a half-buried tortoise shell.

The subterranean command post was manned by a crew of two. Deputy Sheriff Emil Benedict was the senior partner, the man in charge. His subordinate was Assistant Deputy Clem Sugarland. They were monitoring the above-ground scene on the viewscreens of the control panel console. They had been on full alert since the moment the remote sensors first flashed warning of an unidentified airborne being vectored out of the predawn darkness toward the station.

Benedict and Sugarland were in their battle stations. Even an insignificant outpost such as this could defend itself with multilaunch rocket batteries, high-explosive artillery shells, machine Q-guns armed with ion-charged and fragmentation pellets, and electronic warfare (EW) capabilities. The structure itself was hardened against enemies, thick-walled, with the entire central shaft mounted on massive coiled-spring shock absorbers to minimize the concussive impact of a direct hit.

But if the bulky aerial intruder were the spearhead of an attack, it was a ploy unlike any the lawmen had ever seen or heard of. They held their fire as the scanned object's image resolved itself on the screens:

A steel cage filled with what the computerized automatic target recognizer (ATR) identified as "viable bio-units"— that is, live human beings—was being ferried toward the station by a low-flying MagLev suspensor freight barge. Hovering eight to ten feet above the ground on unseen magnetic force fields, the barge drifted stationward with a slow, stately progress not unlike that of an old-time dirigible.

The station was buried in the ground at the northern end of Main Street, which ran north-south. The broad thoroughfare was crossed by the east-west highway connecting San Antonio with Del Rio. The town of Beamer Junction, such as it was, and it wasn't much, was centered around the crossroads. The inhabitants had abandoned the streets at the first sign of trouble, barricading themselves behind the bulletproof shutters and blast-resistant walls of their homes to await the outcome of this bizarre incident.

The suspensor barge glided up Main Street, settling to a landing on the plaza fifty feet away from the station.

"Well, I'll be double-dipped!" Deputy Sheriff Benedict said, staring in disbelief at the viewscreens' multiple close-ups of the hapless prisoners penned in the cage.

"If you're seeing things, then so am I," Assistant Deputy Clem Sugarland said.

"Give us some audio."

Clem threw switches and turned dials, until an exterior directional microphone picked up the clamor inside the cage. A many-voiced torrent of noise came pouring out of the console speaker grids, a babble of bloodcurdling threats and mind-staggering promises of riches. Threats or promises, the ultimate goal was the same: to escape from the cage.

Benedict zoomed in one of the spy-eye cameras to focus on a particular prisoner. A facial close-up of a shaggy-haired, red-bearded giant filled the screen. Glowering from under tufted eyebrows, he sneered with infinite disgust at his fellows and himself.

"My Lord, is that really *Mars Barton*?!"

"Sure looks like him," Clem said.

"*Oh my Lord*—"

"Looks like he's been in a fight, too. See them powder burns and scorch marks on him? And look at that black eye! Somebody sure pasted one on him to leave him with that big black shiner. Man, I'd sure like to meet the hombre who hung that one on him!"

"Me, too—so I could wring his damn fool neck!"

"Huh?" Clem frowned, puzzled. "I don't get it. Barton's one of the most wanted men in the state—heck, in the whole Southwest, and Mexico, too! He's been getting away with murder for years—"

"Yeah," Benedict said. "Why'd he have to turn up on *my* doorstep?"

" 'Turn up'? I'd say it looks more like he was delivered, served up to us on a silver platter—though how that was done is a mystery to me. Anyhow, whoever done it ain't here to stake his claim, which means that we get to split the reward money. Ol' Mars has got a high price on his head. We're gonna be rich, Mr. Benedict!"

"What good's being rich if you're dead?"

" . . . Say again?"

"Barton's been getting away with murder for years because he was supposed to. He's a top hired killer who's laid down hits for some of the biggest names in the state, and I mean B-I-G big, boy. They're not going to sit back and wait for his testimony to put them all in the death chamber. They'll come for him!"

"Shucks, I've been risking my neck on this job just to keep my meal ticket on-line. Reckon I can stand some trouble when there's a big payday to be won."

"Big talk," Benedict said. "You'll change your tune when Mars's pals show up here to bust him out. Those killers have weps you never even heard of, ones that could crack this station like an eggshell. This glorified gopher hole wasn't made to hold the likes of him."

"Or nobody else, hardly."

"What the hell's that supposed to mean?!" the deputy shouted, red-faced.

"Don't mean nothing at all, Mr. Benedict," Clem said with an expression of open-faced innocence.

"By Gawd, if that's an accusation, come out and say it to my face instead of pussyfooting around it!"

"You got me stumped, Mr. Benedict, sir. Accusations? About what? You're my boss. What would I accuse you of?"

"Why—why, nothing, of course!"

"Naturally," Clem agreed. "It ain't your fault that so many prisoners crash out of the holding pens."

"Equipment failure was proved, *proved* to be the cause in each and every jailbreak! You can't hang that on me."

"Sure."

"You're so smart, Sugarland, suppose you go to Sheriff Thornton and ask him to send us some hardware that really works, for a change."

"Well, no, Mr. Benedict, I don't believe I'll do that."

"You're damned right you won't, and I'll tell you why. Because if you did, Thornton would chew you a new asshole, boy! The county's barely got the juice to keep this post open and pay our salaries. You go down to the commissioners courthouse with a mouthful of gimmes and a handful of complaints and they'll toss you out on your ear. They'd just as soon close down this station as not, and if they do, we'll both be out of a job. I don't know about you, but I'm too old to have to go to work for a living."

"Speaking of Sheriff Thornton, shouldn't we contact HQ, let 'em know what's happening?"

"Let's get the situation under control first," Benedict said.

Inputting new commands into the surveillance system, he ordered one of the topside spy-eye cameras to execute a slow pan from face to face across the mass of caged men. The display flowed across the multiscreen monitors.

"Who else is in the bird cage besides Barton?" he asked, sitting hunched forward, squinting at a screen.

"That sad-eyed fellow with the mustache looks a little like Homicide Roldan," Clem said.

"Hell, it is him! He was supposed to have been killed somewhere down in Mexico last year . . ."

The spy-eye moved on to the next man, and the next, unrolling a rogue's gallery across the screens. Outlaws, gangsters, racketeers—killers all. And no small fry. To a man they were all certified public enemies.

"The FBI must've done it," Clem said at last, a bit dazed. "They're the only outfit around with the smarts and firepower to round up this bunch."

"It wasn't them. If this was a fedgov show, they wouldn't be wasting their time with the likes of us. They'd be too busy hogging all the glory for themselves. No, it's not federal," Benedict said.

"Maybe it's a trap," he added, after a pause.

"Mighty expensive bait, Mr. Benedict. Who'd go to the trouble of rounding up some of the most dangerous criminals in Texas just to trap you and me? Heck, it'd be a lot cheaper just to drop a bomb on us."

"That probably comes next."

"Where there's traps there's usually trappers, but danged if I can find any," Clem said.

"That doesn't mean they're not out there, just that you can't find them. Besides which, this horseshit old hardware we're saddled with couldn't find a prairie fire if it was in the middle of it."

"All clear on the proximity range finder. No aircraft, land cars, spy rays, energy flows, nothing," Clem reported. "No people, either, except for the prisoners."

"Sure, the locals are all dug in in their holes, waiting for the deal to go down so they'll know which way to jump. They'd just as soon see us blasted to kingdom come, the bastards."

"Oh, I don't know about that. I've met a few nice folks in town."

"You must've been looking through a microscope to find them. Why, when Jonesy was killed—Jonesy was your predecessor here as assistant deputy—"

"I know who he is. Was," Clem said.

"He was killed a while back, murdered in the line of

duty while protecting the public, mind you. Well, the good people of Beamer Junction didn't even chip in to pay for the funeral. He'd have gone to the body shops to be sold for spare parts if I hadn't stepped in and financed the burial myself. Paid for it out of my own pocket, too."

"That was real big of you, Mr. Benedict."

"Damned straight. But do you think that Sheriff High and Mighty Thornton would authorize the department to reimburse my expenses for seeing to it that a brother officer got a decent send-off? In a pig's ear, he would."

"Poor old Jonesy," Clem said. "Got killed in one of them jailbreaks, didn't he?"

"That's right. Want to make something out of it?"

"No, sir. I just don't want to make the same mistake he did, whatever that was."

"He started thinking he was deputy sheriff material."

"Oh."

Shrugging, Clem switched on a wave-pulse generator and triggered a burst. Topside, a funnel-shaped projector fired an energy beam at the cage. The beam was invisible, but the prisoners could feel it, an unseen force that tingled their flesh, rattled their bones, and made their hair stand on end. Some of them started shouting and screaming.

The beamed wave-pulse was harmless to flesh and blood, but would instantly activate the detonator of any bomb in its path, causing it to explode. A useful device for dealing with concealed logic-chip "smart" bombs and mines, booby traps, and other infernal machines.

No bombs were planted among the prisoners, the cage, or its environs. Otherwise the beam sweep would have set them off with a blast.

The prisoners who had panicked settled down and fell silent when they realized they were going to live, for a little while longer, at least.

"Chickenshits," Mars Barton said, sneering at the four of his fellow prisoners who had succumbed to stark fear. It was the first word he had spoken since waking up hours earlier to find himself bruised, battered, and behind bars.

"If there was a bomb aboard we'd have all been blown

to atoms long before you could even feel the wave beam," he said. "Dumbasses."

"You don't look so smart yourself, caged up in here like the rest of us," Marco said. He was sharp-faced, jockey-sized.

"I'm going to kill you for that."

"Yeah? How, by remote control?"

"Every man, woman, and child I ever put on my list died. Every one. You're on my list, Marco."

"Big man. Let's see how tough you are when they seal you into that death chamber, big boy."

"No jail can hold the Red Planet Man."

"Big talk."

"I'm going to kill you, Marco."

"All you big guys are yellow down deep, when the crunch comes. It's a known fact," Marco said.

"Shut up, both of you pigs," Homicide Roldan said.

"You're dead," Barton said, not skipping a beat. "I'm going to kill you for calling me a pig, Roldan."

"I kill you first, you pig."

"Save it for the guy who put us in here," somebody said.

That gave them all something to think about. Gloom fell on the group, silence. Mars Barton was the first to break the hush.

"I'll kill him, too, the longest and hardest kill of them all," the Martian said. "Only—who is he?"

"That's what we'd all like to know," Action Man Blugeld said.

"You're the guy with all the answers, Skintop. Any ideas as to who put the arm on us?" Marco said.

Skintop was hairless from head to toe, with a pear-shaped face and a physique to match.

"I'm as much in the dark as the rest of you boys, but I can tell you this," he said. "Whoever he is, this mystery man's no friend of ours."

"No shit, Sherlock. I figured that one out by myself," Marco said.

"Then what'd you ask me for?"

"I know who he is," Niles Visser said.

"Bullshit," Marco said.

Addiction to the dangerous synthetic hormone Ferol had turned the whites of Visser's eyes red and his gums purple. His yellow teeth had been filed into sharp points. As a member of the Chrome Mau Mau secret society, he followed their custom of cutting a notch in his ears for each of his kills. He had had so many kills that both of his ears were fringed on the edge all the way around. It would not be pleasant when his current dose of Ferol began to wear off, but the redness of his eyes indicated that that time was yet to come.

"I know," he said.

"Yeah? How about letting the rest of us in on the secret?"

"He's the Man, Marco."

"What kind of jiveass double-talk is that?!"

"The Man, Sam, that's what he am. The Man with a plan. Law man, gun man, kick-ass man. The Man."

"He sure whomped our butts," somebody said.

"That's why he's the Man," Visser said. "The Big Boss Man."

"Somebody's got to go topside and you're elected, Sugarland."

"I'll be done suiting up in a minute, Mr. Benedict."

"No hurry. Those crooks aren't going anywhere. Let them stew for a while, it's good for them. The heat will cook some of the poison out of them."

Benedict occupied the command chair of the control console. Rows of instrument panels were set back in steps atop the massive mechanism, stacked like the keyboards of an old-fashioned church pipe organ. Two tiers of viewscreens rose from the top of the console.

Benedict fingered the handgrips of his set of controls for the weapons firing system. The safeties were on, Clem noticed, while trying to seem as if he weren't paying attention to such things.

"I'll cover you from here with the big guns," Benedict

said. "If it's a trap, I'll open up and turn those crooks into chopped meat!"

Slowed by battle armor, Clem clumped to his customary sideman spot at the console and ponderously lowered himself into the chair.

"This is no time to be sitting down on the job," Benedict said.

"Can't fix these battle boots standing up."

Reaching down, Clem began fiddling with the adjustable straps and buckles of his cumbersome antishock boots.

"Reach headquarters yet?" he asked.

"No, I'm still trying to get through."

"That's funny, they were coming through loud and clear just a few hours ago."

"Signals are always stronger at night. Maybe a local magnetic storm is blocking our transmission. Or maybe it's a glitch somewhere in our equipment. I'll attend to it directly."

"I'd sure feel a whole lot better if HQ was in on this thing, just in case something goes wrong. At least then we'd have our asses covered with the higher-ups."

"Hell, boy, if something goes wrong you won't have any ass left to cover! But don't worry. From where I sit, we've got the situation under control."

"From where you sit—yeah."

"Senior man's always the last to leave his post, Sugarland. That's departmental standard operating procedure."

"It's also SOP to report any unusual activity to headquarters ASAP. And if having ten big-shot crooks drop in on us out of the blue ain't unusual, I don't know what is!"

"ASAP means As Soon As Possible, Sugarland. I can't report until the comm system starts cooperating again."

"Why don't I give it a try? I'm a pretty fair hand with a broadcast beam, if I do say so myself."

Clem started to rise from his chair, but Benedict motioned for him to sit back down.

"Finish what you're doing. You've got important work

to do topside. I'll give headquarters another try."

"Okay."

Benedict swiveled his chair to the left so he was facing the comm system's instrument board. He fiddled with switches and turned dials, producing a variety of electronic wheeps, beeps, and whoops that were counterpointed with the wash of hissing static coming through the speaker grids. He sat in such a way that his body blocked Clem's view of what his hands were really doing on the controls.

But that put his back to Clem, too, so he couldn't see what his assistant was doing. Glancing sideways to make sure that Benedict was fully occupied, Clem reached down as if to readjust the fastenings of his boots. Instead, he ran his fingers along the underside of the console's overhanging kneehole flange until he found a small stud, about the size of a nailhead. He pressed it. A hinged lid swung open and downward, exposing a recessed space that was roughly the size and shape of a brick. The lid unlatched with a click, but Benedict didn't hear it over the surflike noise of the static.

The space was a fusebox, one of a row of them located for easy access under the console overhang. Making sure that Benedict was still occupied with the balky communicator (or pretending to be), Clem reached into the box and removed a few key fuses, tiny clear plastic tubes with hairlike wire filament cores. Palming the fuses, he closed the fusebox lid and straightened up in his seat. Benedict was none the wiser.

"Any luck reaching HQ?" Clem said.

"I'm making progress," Benedict said over his shoulder. He lowered the volume control, muting the static to a low background hiss.

"The interference seems to be dying down. Probably a local mag storm, like I said. I should be able to punch through a beam in a few more minutes," he said. "Ready to go topside, Sugarland?"

"Yes, sir."

"Well, get to it, then. I want to be able to tell HQ that we've got the situation well in hand."

Clem rose, making for the armory at the opposite end of the command post. He crossed the circular floor of the station's cylindrically shaped central core, his heavy footfalls echoing through the silo-like shaft. Battle armor restricted his movements, causing him to move in a loose-jointed, shambling stance with his heavy-booted feet spread far apart to maintain better balance.

A sidelong glimpse of the comm system board confirmed his suspicions: the settings were all wrong to send a transceiver beam to headquarters. Benedict was just going through the motions, pretending to be trying to send a message.

Two can play at that game, Clem thought, feeling the filched fuses nestled comfortably in the palm of his left hand.

He input the armory access code on a keypad, unlocking the ponderous hatch door. The armory was built like a bank vault—better, in fact, since weapons were more valuable than money in the savage world of A.D. 2035.

Unsealed, the massive door swung outward and open. It was six feet in diameter and three feet thick, made of compound layers of metalloy and super-strength ceramics. Clem had to duck his head as he stepped through the hatchway into the vault. Long guns and hand weapons hung in racks on the walls; floor bins held quantities of cartridges, replacement charge clips, special task rounds, bolt-on laser target-finders, and other lethal options. A separate case stored a variety of crowd-control shells: gas, irritant powder, blister fog, Vomex, sub- and hyper-sonic "screamer" pellets. A few extra battle armor suits hung on hooks on the back wall, and a tripod-mounted light machine gun sat on the floor in the corner. All the station's conwep—conventional weaponry—was here, except for the Q-gun ammunition, which was stored in the big gun's turret.

Clem put the fuses in a safe place in the medikit box clipped to his utility belt. He then armed himself with an assault rifle, equipped with an underslung shock-charge beamer, and a holstered pair of machine pistols, which he belted onto his hips. To his utility belt he secured a bulletproof box, filled with spare ammo clips, and two grenades, one smoke and one flash-concussion. Almost as an afterthought, he added a high explosive (HE) grenade to his armaments.

Slinging the rifle over his shoulder and holding a helmet under one arm, he exited the armory vault and resealed it.

"Nothing new to report, except that our caged birds are getting a whole hell of a lot hotter now that the sun's coming up," Benedict said.

Seeing Clem eyeing the transceiver, he added, "I had HQ for a few seconds but I lost them. That mag storm must be a big one."

"Must be."

Clem ran a commo check on the mini-transceiver built into his helmet. It worked fine. Donning the helmet, he secured the bottom of it to the notches and grooves of the ring collar of his armored torso protector. A slight turn to the left locked it in place with an airtight seal. He kept his visored face-plate raised, not wanting to tap into the suit's canned air until the last possible second.

"Well, here goes nothing," he said.

"Cheer up! Think of how much worse it would be if you had to go up against any one of those fellows if he wasn't caged. Besides, if things work out, you're going to be a rich man. We both will. You can use your share of the reward to buy your own station and then you can be the boss," Benedict said.

Clem picked up his gauntlets and crossed to the elevator. A spiral staircase wound around a central axis pillar to the upper levels, but it was basically an auxiliary fallback option in case an emergency should incapacitate the elevators.

Clem pressed a button, the doors opened, and he entered the car. He pressed another button to go to the top level.

"There's a commendation in this for you for sure, maybe even a medal," Benedict was calling to him as the elevator doors slid shut.

Clem stepped off at the top floor, the car doors automatically *whooshing* shut behind him. He was in a loftlike space, a single room whose ceiling was the curved dome at the top of the station which protruded above ground. No windows broke the uniformity of its smooth walls, to maintain the greatest structural integrity against bombs, bullets, beams, and burners. Viewscreens on a console rising from the floor at the center of the room were video windows on the outside world.

Clem fitted his hands inside the gauntlets, whose tops fastened to the ring cuffs of the fleximesh sleeves of his armor, forming an airtight seal to protect against airborne toxic agents.

He lowered his face-plate, his suit's self-contained oxy supply switching on the instant that the visor was sealed into place. The bottled air was oxygen-enriched but tasted flat with that stale, "canned" flavor given it by the high-compression tanks. It sure beat inhaling a double lungful of deadly nerve gas or viral bio-spray, though.

Pausing to finetune the helmet's audionics, he boosted the pickup on the exterior mikes and lowered the volume of Benedict's transmissions.

He went to the airlock opposite the elevator from which he had emerged. The dogs unlocked; the hatch opened. Clem entered the chamber. The hatch closed and the autodogs battened down, locking it.

The airlock was similar in size and shape to an old-fashioned diving bell. The terror tactics of the times demanded that any paramilitary installation that wanted to stay in business must be protected against contamination from Chemical and Biological Warfare agents. CBW had been used extensively in most of the major and minor global conflicts of the last forty years. A lot of CBW surplus hardware was left over from the last war, and it wasn't that hard to make from scratch, either.

Pumps chugged as the airlock began cycling. Red warning lights shone as the air was sucked out of the chamber. Pneumatic tubes veining Clem's bodysuit like a circulatory system inflated, compensating for the decrease in air pressure. Still, the sensation was uncomfortable. Not for the first time, Clem thought about how the airlock would make a pretty fair death chamber, especially since the controls could be overridden by the station's command console down below.

That was why he had brought along the HE grenade. If for some reason the hatches refused to open, as a last resort he could blast them open with the grenade. Who knows? He might even survive the explosion, thanks to his armor.

But there were no tricks, no surprises. High-pitched whistling sounded as the outside air was gradually bled into the low-pressure chamber. The unpleasant sensation lessened until pressure was restored to normal.

His suit-mounted sensors detected no traces of CBW toxic agents in the outer air, leaving the helmet's internal warning buzzer unsounded and the alarm lights unlit. Good. But he was keeping his suit sealed. He had never had to suit up to this extent to go topside before, except for a few rare occasions when the station was on full battle alert— false alerts.

And this time?

Green go lights flashed on the display board over the top of the hatch, replacing the red lights. Clem threw the release. The hatch unhooked and swung up and outward, opening on a passageway, a slab-sided corridor about ten feet long and eight feet high. The muzzle of Clem's shoulder-slung rifle missed grazing the ceiling by a few inches. Overhead, inset disc-shaped glow panels spaced at regular intervals shed a watery, cheerless light.

The corridor ended in a massive metal portal. Clem activated the unlocking mechanism. Hidden motors, unseen but heard, lowered the foot-thick blast-proof door out and down, like a drawbridge. Meanwhile, Clem had slung down his rifle so that he held it waist-high in both hands, leveling the muzzle.

The drawbridge touched ground, settling itself lengthwise with the dull thudding boom of a couple of tons of metal nestling into terra firma.

Clem stepped outside, into the open.

THREE

NICE DAY, CLEM thought.

The sun had been up for over an hour, and the temperature was only ninety-seven degrees Fahrenheit. South Texas had always been traditionally hot, but this was different. Global warming trends had expanded the equatorial torrid zone northward and southward, with cataclysmic results. One minor consequence was that South and East Texas, and the other Gulf Coast states, now experienced a subtropical climate, sultry and wet. Most of the Florida interior was said to be impenetrable rain forest, as was the Louisiana bayou country and Texas's own Big Thicket. Information was sketchy, since communication had largely ceased from those areas and few investigators who ventured into the green domains ever returned to report.

In Southwest Texas, the tropical heat and humidity were offset somewhat by the scorching Scorpion Wind that blew hot dry air from the newly made desert Badlands on both sides of the border. Beamer Junction lay in this zone, and so suffered the extremes of both dry and wet weather, often on the same day.

Today the Scorpion Wind had subsided, replaced by heavy moisture-laden air from the Gulf. Haze dimmed the sun, lowering the heat. Not much, though.

Coin-sized micro-refrigeration units were strategically placed at key "hot points" in the bodysuit under Clem's armor. Without them he would have keeled over and cooked in his own juices in a few minutes. With them he felt as if he were wrapped in hot towels from head to toe, but at least he could function for a while.

He moved forward to take a closer look at the prisoners. But not too close. Some of them ignored him; others cursed or cajoled him.

The cage was crude but effective, a boxlike construction of gridded metal bars. A soft scrap metal, steel probably, which was soft indeed compared to the newer metalloys and compound laminates, but hard enough to pen the toughest flesh and blood. The sections had been fused together by an industrial burner, standard equipment at any major construction site, of which there were none in Beamer Junction.

Sets of chains and mag-clamp binders secured the cage to the freight bed of the suspensor barge. The driver's cab amidships on the starboard side was untenanted, but that meant nothing. Barges were most often guided to their preprogrammed destinations by an autonomic computer guidance system. In this way they could be linked together in great convoy caravans similar to the freight trains of another time. The driver's cab controls allowed the vehicle to be manually operated if necessary.

In this case, while outside the limit of its detectors, someone had input the substation as the barge's destination. He—or she, or they—could have been long gone while the barge was still cruising on robot pilot toward its target. That seemed to be what had happened, but Clem reminded himself to accept nothing at face value in this case.

The prisoners were a sorry-looking lot, by and large, but they still had plenty of piss and vinegar in them. Ten men, hard-used, disarmed, their clothes in tatters, all crowded into a metal-grilled box. They lined the walls, sitting with their backs to the metal and their legs stretched out flat across the floor. They were manacled to the bars, presumably so they couldn't get at each other, since manacles or no manacles they weren't going to get out. Whatever opening in the framework had allowed them to enter the cage had been welded shut when the last man was in place. It would take a heavy-duty burner or industrial-strength cutting tool to free them.

Clem was in no hurry to do that.

They were quite a collection: Armando "Homicide" Roldan, pistolero for the Mexicrime mobs north and south of the border; Tony Calamari, impresario of homicidal entertainments; Doc Endocrine, Frankenscientist; Niles Visser, murder cultist and killer for hire who combined work and worship; Tranh Vanh, number three man of the Vietnamese BTK gang's vice operations in the Badlands mining towns; Bilko Skintop, confidence trickster, macro-swindler supreme; Enro Blugeld, extremist, death squad organizer for Bill Braun's GodSword order; Mars Barton the Red Planet Man, corporate assassin; and Marco and Johnson, two-thirds of the Three Gents goon squad—less than two-thirds now, technically, since there wasn't all that much left of Johnson.

Ten one-man crime waves.

If this was some kind of a trap, it was none of their doing. Their shared sense of outrage at having been caught was real and raw. Besides, what conspiracy could have gathered ten such disparate individuals under one roof?

The prisoners wanted out:

"Free me and I'll make you rich," Squid Tony said.

"A harem of beautiful virgins. You'll be their lord and master, with the power of life or death over them. You'll have wealth, a new identity in the pleasure city of your choice. All you have to do is set me free," Tranh Vanh said.

"My compadres will kill the one you love the most if you don't let me go," Roldan said.

"How'd you like to stay the same age you are now for the next fifty, one hundred years? I can fix it so you do!" said Doc Endocrine.

"Let me go or I'll kill you." That from Mars Barton.

Others offered minor variations on similar themes. All spoke at once, a chaotic clamor.

"If that don't beat all," Clem said, shaking his head.

The big question: who had rounded up the crooks?

Earlier:

Duncan, Marco, and Johnson were known as the Three Gents goon squad, adept at extortion, debt collecting, strong-arm violence, and murder. Duncan was a mannerly killer, the kind who says "After you" when escorting a victim to the murder site. He was a puffy-faced drunk with lynx eyes, the brains of the operation. Marco drove and handled the legwork. He was a wiseguy and a sharp dresser. Johnson was the muscle, a hulking nightmare figure with hands as big as catcher's mitts. A dim-witted sadist, he knew enough to keep his mouth shut and follow orders.

A synthetic foods magnate wanted to be rid of a county health inspector who was investigating an outbreak of food poisoning that had killed one hundred and fifty people. It was a fluke, a one-of-a-kind accident that had fatally contaminated a vat of liquid foodstuffs. The problem area was pinpointed and remedied, and safeguards were put in place to guarantee against a repetition of the tragedy. That should have satisfied the inspector, but he didn't know to leave well enough alone. So the magnate farmed the problem out to the Three Gents for final disposition.

The marked man's ground car was sabotaged so that it broke down at night on the road to Ventralia, while he was returning from a visit to a processing plant outside the city. The trio was trailing close behind in a company van stolen from the facility.

The stricken machine lurched, fishtailed, recovered. It rolled to a dead halt on a lonely stretch of roadway, deserted as far as the eye could see. The pavement was cracked and there were no streetlights. Ventralia lay hidden beyond the next, distant ridge.

Marco pulled the van in at the side of the road a few dozen yards behind the car. Duncan and Johnson got out of the cab and started toward the stalled vehicle, splitting up to approach it from both sides. The plan was simple: kill the mark, load the body in the back of the van. Duncan would drive the car into the city and abandon it in some quiet part of town, to make it look as though the mark had made it to Ventralia before vanishing. Marco and Johnson would return to the processing plant, unload the corpse from the van, dispose of it in the shredders and grinders of the liqui-protein intake ports, and escape in the getaway car hidden on the premises. Not so coincidentally, the plant was secretly owned by the synthi-foods magnate who had hired them in the first place.

That was the plan. It started to go sour when Johnson, nearing the car on the passenger side, said, "Hey, there's nobody in there!"

"Impossible," Duncan said, closing in on the driver's side. But Johnson was right; the driver was nowhere to be seen.

Duncan crouched, wary, senses tingling, heart pounding. Maybe the mark had figured out the score and ducked down below the windows, trying to hide. Duncan didn't like that so well. He didn't fancy poking around the car to discover that the mark was inside and maybe had a gun, too.

"Go look in the car," he told Johnson.

"Nope, nobody inside," Johnson reported a moment later.

"All three of us saw him driving the car before. He must have ducked out before we started moving in. He's smarter than I thought but it won't do him any good. He can't have gotten far. We'll find him," Duncan said.

"We'd better find him," he added, worried.

No other vehicles were on the roadway. Flat weedy ground stretched out on both sides. No buildings. The sky was overcast, hiding the stars. Warm breezes blew streamers of dirt across the road.

Marco leaned out of the cab, saying, "What's wrong?"

"Shut up," Duncan said. Switching his blaster to his left hand, he pulled an infrared detector from his pocket. The hand-held device was an oblong box with a sensor grid covering one of its short ends.

Johnson stood knee-deep in weeds a few yards from the road's edge, squinting into the darkness.

"Get out of the way," Duncan told him, gesturing with the IR detector. "The heatseeker will find him no matter how well he's hidden."

"I hear something moving out there, Dunc—"

There was a muffled report, a thud, and then Johnson was enveloped in a crackling blue cloud of light.

A web of spidery blue lightning wrapped Johnson from head to toe, immobilizing him. Shadows were jet black in the blue-white glare. A heartbeat later, the blue cloud ceased to exist, swiftly fading into nothingness.

Johnson was knocked to the ground. The air filled with a smell of ozone, overheated circuitry, melted insulation.

Duncan flattened himself on the pavement, sheltering behind the car. He knew what had happened. Johnson had been hit by a pulsed shock charge projectile launched by an unseen foe. Releasing its energy on contact, a pulsed charge shorted out all the target's EMG (electro-magnetic) hardware and defenses as well as rendering him unconscious.

A lousy health inspector didn't pack that kind of high-tech firepower! What was going on here?

Duncan scuttled around, crablike, seeking cover and the enemy at the same time. The car's metal mass would shield him from shock charges, as long as he didn't stay too close to it.

Marco hopped down from the cab, gun in hand. Dropping to one knee, he took cover behind the front tire, made of nonconductive solid rubber. He was armed with an unregistered burner, a restricted class one energy weapon, possession of which was a federal offense. Like its wielder, the burner was small, efficient, deadly. Its pencil-thin ray of ultraviolet light could bore a hole through an inch-thick metalloy armor plate. Most effective when used at close quarters, within a range of thirty feet or less, it could kill an unshielded adult within twenty-five yards.

Johnson lay flat on his back, convulsing, tendrils of smoke rising from the scorch marks on his clothes.

Another mini-missile came whizzing out of the darkness. Unlike the one that had hit Johnson, it did not carry a shock charge, but was instead armed with an explosive micro-tip.

It impacted the car with a crash and a boom, flipping it on its side, then overturning it. The car fell on Duncan, flattening him like a bug being pressed by a hot steam iron.

The concussion picked up Johnson, tossing him into the middle of the road. The blast must have jarred him to his senses, because he clenched his fists and tried to sit up.

Marco thought he had glimpsed where the shot came from, but when he triggered a heat ray in that direction, the bomb blast had thrown off his aim.

Marco had had enough. He would have stayed and fought it out to the end, no matter what, if there had been even the slightest chance that Duncan would survive. He would have done so out of fear, not loyalty. But Duncan was dead and Marco had no fear of deserting Johnson. Without Duncan to tell him what to do, the moronic man-mountain couldn't find his nose at the end of his face.

Johnson was tough. Tough, or just too stupid to know when he was licked. He stood on his knees in the road now, fighting to throw off a jolt that would have left a normal-sized man unconscious.

Marco's musings were cut short by a blur of motion in the field between the car and the van. He fired at heat ray at it. The magenta ray ripped through the air with a sound like tearing silk.

It missed. Marco didn't wait for the counterpunch. He leaped, throwing himself away from the van in a head-first dive.

An explosive mini-missile hit the van broadside, smashing it into a ball of red-hot metal. Pressure waves flung Marco head over heels through the air. He didn't know which end was up, but he held on to the burner.

He hit the pavement when he didn't expect to, hit it hard, bounced, rolled to a stop. He was dazed, battered, partially deafened by the blasts, but he still had the burner.

Smoke from the burning vehicles stung his eyes, choked him. He lay sprawled on his side, eyes tearing. He coughed, gasped, and wheezed as hot oily smoke swirled around him.

Footsteps sounded, scuffing on pavement. They had to be very close for Marco to hear them over the ringing in his ears. Wiping smoke-irritated eyes with the back of his hand, he sat up and tried to look everywhere at once.

A hulking form loomed out of the smoke, coming toward him. Marco switched the ray aperture setting to wide fan, squeezed the trigger so hard it hurt, and held it down.

The ray sounded like a blowtorch now. It hit its target low, cutting off his left leg just above the knee. The figure took another step forward, then collapsed. The big left shoe, with most of the severed leg still in it, stood upright for an instant, then toppled. There was surprisingly little gore, since the heat ray had cauterized the wound even while performing the amputation.

Johnson crashed to earth a few yards from where Marco lay. There was less smoke near the ground, letting them see each other by firelight. Marco shrieked.

"I'm sorry, I didn't know it was you, I swear!" he cried.

Johnson looked at him, glanced at the still-smoldering stump of his left thigh, looked at Marco again, and started crawling toward him.

"Keep away from me—"

Johnson dragged himself across the pavement, as ungainly as a walrus wriggling over an ice floe. He reached out for Marco with big strangler's hands.

Marco fired at almost point-blank range, lopping off the right hand that Johnson had held raised above his head, poised to strike. Marco had been shooting at the head, but he'd aimed high. The severed hand plopped palm-up on the roadway.

Marco forgot to release the trigger and drained the last reserves of the depleted power cell. The ray darkened, streaked, then dimmed to a cone of dull purple light too weak to inflict even a mild sunburn.

Still game, Johnson kept on coming, crawling, clawing at Marco with his one good hand. Marco froze.

Johnson's fist clubbed Marco's shoulder, numbing it. He grabbed Marco by the neck, overpowering the other man's feeble attempts to fend him off. Johnson's fingers closed around Marco's throat, squeezing, choking the life out of him.

A figure came into view a few paces from them. A man. He was big, taller even than Johnson, though not so heavy. His features were vague, indistinct, formless in the swirling smoke.

The stranger held a gun, a short, stubby, wicked-looking weapon. A mini-missile launcher.

He fired a shock charge into Johnson's broad back at close range. The blue cloud blanketed the maimed titan, and Marco, too.

By the time Marco got the charge, though, it had been filtered through Johnson, which robbed it of some of its strength. It still packed a punch. Intolerable brightness exploded inside Marco's head. For one awful instant, he felt as if his skeleton were trying to tear itself free from his body.

He blacked out . . .

When he came to, he found himself in the cage, chained to the bars. His despair was complete when a quick self-survey revealed that he had been expertly stripped of all the hideaway weapons he'd concealed on his garments and person. He'd been defanged and declawed, tamed.

Caught.

Johnson was there, too, or at least what was left of him. He was comatose, in shock, near death, but perhaps his unquenchable brute vitality would pull him through, saving him for legal execution in the death chamber. Critical condition or not, Johnson, too, was in chains, with his remaining hand manacled to the bars. Their mysterious captor, whoever he was, was taking no chances . . .

Tony Calandria was born into a family of third-generation nuclear waste disposal technicians, which may have been why he had flippers instead of arms. An uncle of his was a mid-level member of the Atomic Byproducts Processors National Council, so the guild members' free clinic fitted the youngster with prosthetic attachments to serve as his arms and hands. The cyborged appliances were upgraded and replaced every few years to keep up with the growing boy. His agile mind was strengthened by hardship and warped by the cruelties that the vicious inflict on those who are different. That toughness of mind, combined with artificial hydraulic-powered arms that could dismember a fully grown adult as easily as picking the petals off a flower, made Tony a very dangerous individual who made his mark in crime at an early age. He moved fast, and when he reached the top of his particular profession, he celebrated his swift rise by outfitting himself with the finest set of artificial arms that money could buy. Then he spent more money having the prosthetic devices customized into deadly killing weapons. They were periodically made more elaborate, incorporating ever-more complex and frightful modifications, such as rotary saws, drills, dart guns, flame jets, even a burner in his right arm and a beamer in his left.

Some anonymous wit dubbed him Tony Calamari, Tony the Squid, and the tag stuck. The originator of the phrase was wise to remain unknown, because at first Tony would have pureed his face with the triple-bladed high-speed rotary drill built into one of his mechanical appendages. Later, after giving it some thought, Tony decided he liked the nickname. A showman first and foremost, he realized the marquee value of his unique attachments. More than a few paying customers attended his exhibitions as much to see the fabled promotor as to witness the meets.

Tony was an impresario, a presenter of special events that combined the ultra-violence of the old-time Roman gladiatorial combats with the show business savvy of today. He liked to claim that he was part of an honored tradition of savage entertainment that included such illustrious forebears as bullfights, bear baiting, public executions, hockey fights, professional wrestling, demolition derbies, and snuff movies. Blood sports were his stock in trade.

Only a few days ago, he had been presenting Tony's Cockfight Meet, the latest in a series of such contests that had been enjoying a spectacular success on tour of the Crescent Cities bordering the Badlands, where life was cheap and good entertainment was hard to come by. This particular contest was being held in an unusual venue, an old abandoned oil storage tank a few miles outside

Middletown. Cockfighting was illegal in Texas, as well as every other state in the union, which only increased its potency as an audience draw. As always, Tony solved the problem by bribing the necessary officials, especially in local law enforcement. His advance men handed out free passes at the police station, and bought some extra goodwill by hiring off-duty cops to handle crowd control at the contest.

Local interest ran high and the event was a sold-out success. Before nightfall, scores of multi-vehicle convoys started streaming out of the city toward the contest site. For many, it was a rare venture outside Middletown's protected perimeter. For this night only, security outside city walls was guaranteed, thanks to the protection of the police and the local crime bosses, who had also been well greased. Safe passage to and from the venue was also personally guaranteed by Tony himself, whose bloodthirsty vindictiveness was well known. The word went out to Middletown's legions of bandits, hijackers, heisters, and highwaymen: *Lay off.* Violators would be vaporized.

A city of lights came into being at dusk on the desolate industrial wasteland northeast of Middletown, created by the headlights, taillights, and running lights of the hundreds of vehicles swarming to the contest site. The mood of the crowd was a cross between that of a county fair and a lynching.

To admit the crowd, entrances had been rayed out at strategic places in the sides of the oil storage tank. Many smaller holes had been opened in the structure to ventilate it. A circular pit, fifteen feet deep, had been dug in the center of the floor—the cockpit. Grouped around it in a 270-degree arc were bleachers, rising in a series of tiers overlooking the pit. The bleachers were part of the touring group's permanent equipment, transported from town to town on MagLev floating barges just as the circuses of a happier age had shipped their gear on wagons, trains, and trucks. Lights were hung throughout the vast space, strings of floating glo-globes, spotlights, and floodlights.

The three-quarter amphitheater faced the fourth, back-stage section, used as a technical support and crew area. It was screened off by a thin opaque curtain flown from the roof to the floor, so as not to distract from the action in the cockpit. A long, wide ramp had been dug in the floor backstage, slanting downward to connect with the arena floor. A sliding door like those used in the bull-ring stood between cockpit and ramp as an added safe-ty precaution. For their own safety and that of the pub-lic's (not to mention Tony's and the crew's), the contest-ants were kept penned in SCUs, single confinement units, until it was their time to compete. The SCUs looked like plastic coffins stood upright. Before a match, a forklift would carry the contestants' SCUs, one at a time, down the ramp, under the raised sliding door, and into the cock-pit. They would be placed at opposite ends of the arena, facing each other. Then the forklift operator would get the hell out of the cockpit as fast as he could, the slid-ing gate would drop, and the match would be ready to begin.

In times past, cockfighting had been a blood sport in which fighting cocks—roosters, that is—were set against one another in a fight to the death. The bantams were often fitted with barbed spurs to enliven the action. In the twenty-first century, cockfighting had taken on a somewhat different meaning. The end result was the same, a fight to the death, but the combatants had changed. Roosters were out. Such rare birds were worth their weight in gold, too valuable to waste, assuming they could be found in the first place. In A.D. 2035, poultry was more precious than people. Cockfights used people now, and there was never any shortage of volunteers, even though each entrant had only a fifty-fifty chance of surviving a match. Less than that, since many matches ended with the death of both contestants. The losing contestant's survivors, though, were guaranteed a part of the loot.

Cockfights must not be confused with such traditional sports fare as killboxing, motor polo, auto destruct racing, bungee cord duels, Murder Wrasslin' and its fast-growing spin-off, Masked Murder Wrasslin', and, most popular of all, Official West Hemispheric League Death Football, the number one sport from the Aleuts to Tierra del Fuego for years in a row. These were all legitimate sporting events, duly sanctioned and licensed by their respective governing bodies. Cockfighting still retained the aura of something sleazy and not quite respectable, despite or perhaps because of its great popularity.

The drugging of contestants was the main reason for cockfighting's unsavory image. It was strictly voluntary, and all entrants were required to sign an affidavit to that effect prior to participating. Before the match, they received an airgun injection of a compound serum. The critical ingredient in the mix was a strong dose of Caterol, a highly concentrated derivative of Ferol, the so-called "violence drug" (actually, it was a designer hormone made from glandular extracts). Skilled underground pharmaco-chemists bound a concentrated distillate of Ferol to an enzymatic catalyst, potentiating the Ferol effect a hundredfold.

Those who had taken Caterol once and survived were never the same afterward. A second encounter was usually fatal, a third always, although there was a rumor of a user in Neo-Detroit who had taken it five times and was not only still alive, but could even remember his own name. Still, the odds were in favor of surviving a one-shot exposure. Survive that, and the cockfight, too, and the lucky winner would be paid off on the spot with more credit-units than he or she could expect to earn in a year's worth of honest drone work. The cash prizes were a fractional operating expense to a big-shot promoter like Tony, mere chickenfeed.

The Caterol was mixed with a soup of amphetimines, pain-killers, Adrenalin, and fast-acting synthi-sterries, synthetic steroids. The dosage was time-released so as to not come on all at once, but gradually, to prolong the combat for a better show.

Showmanship was vital to the game. It wasn't enough just to stage eight or ten matches in a row and then bring up the houselights. The public wanted value for money.

Even the most simple folks got bored watching a succession of hopped-up homicidal maniacs battle to the death. You had to give them a *show*. That was Tony's philosophy, and it had made him rich. He knew how to play to the crowd. Each match was unique. Knives, axes, mailed fists, sledgehammers, blow torches, spiked elbow guards and knee pads, Krueger fingerknife gloves, hedge clippers, and shock sticks were only a few of the weapons the cockfighters took into combat. Tony varied the format, too, with unusual combinations: one man against two boys, age versus youth, Family Feuds, Ethnic Hatred Nights, Midget and Dwarf Cockfighting, and that surefire crowd pleaser, Battle of the Sexes.

On the night that Tony met his match, he was backstage, following his usual custom of counting the house before the games began. Another sellout crowd; the stands were packed. And not just with the sporting element—although they were well represented—but also with a fair slice of what passed for respectable folk in town. Day laborers and low-level contract workers filled the upper tiers, middle management exec-caste members filled the middle tiers, and the local gentry enjoyed the best seats in the house. Some of the elite flaunted their glamorous mistresses; virtually all of them were protected by bodyguards. The few who were without such protection were either very rash or very dangerous individuals.

It was hot. It was always hot in this part of the country, night and day; inside the tank it was sweltering. Roustabouts had opened up as many skylights and ventiports as the troupe's engineer calculated the structure could take without weakening to the point of collapse. A battery of four Kwik-Kold refrigerator cannons did little more than agitate the syrupy air. Tony knew how to beat the heat, though: his clothes were studded with micro-refrigeration chips, keeping him delightfully cool. His prosthetic mekarms required their own independent cooling system to offset the heat of their motors.

The show was about to start. The contestants were already armed, armored, injected, and isolated in their SCUs. Once they had been injected ("juiced" in the jargon of the game), they had passed the point of no return. They were outfitted and equipped before the injections, since none of the crew wanted to get near them afterward. Caterol was administered only when the subjects were safely locked in their restraints inside the SCUs. Dosages were individually graded, with time-release buffers, which ensured that contestants in the second half of the program would not feel the full effect of the drug until it was their turn to compete. After the injections, the doors of the SCUs were sealed, not to be opened again until match time.

Showtime. Tony prepared to make his entrance. He descended the ramp, reinforced earthen walls rising above him. The sliding door lifted open, bringing a response from the aficionados in the crowd who knew its significance. The houselights dimmed, and everybody knew what that meant. They roared their approval, a multithroated battle cry of primordial bloodlust. The gentry shouted as loud as anyone.

Expertly milking the response, Tony delayed his entrance while the fans whooped themselves to a peak of frenzy. His savoring of the buildup was soured by a persistent and ever-growing backstage clamor. It was loud indeed, to be heard over the spectators' shouts.

"What's that racket?" he finally said, frowning. He had to shout to be heard by his clique of stooges, who were right beside him. They didn't know what it was, either.

"I'll find out," one of them said, starting up the ramp.

"When you do, put a lid on it," Tony said.

The stooge didn't hear him, but he didn't have to be told what to do. If the boss's opening speech didn't come off without a hitch, there would be hell to pay.

And just what was making all that noise, anyway? Pounding and shouting and shrieking . . . it sounded like a jail-break in Hell.

Backstage was chaos. Crew members stood by help-lessly, not knowing what to do. The stooge froze, too, when the full import of the outburst came crashing in on his brain.

The noise came from the SCUs—from their occupants, who sounded as if they were in the full throes of drug-induced mania. There was always some of that from the contestants as they neared their scheduled events, but nothing like this. They all would have to be peaking at once to produce such chaos.

Which was impossible. That was the whole rationale behind the time-release doses, to prevent this sort of thing. Too many safeguards were in place to allow such a disaster.

Ullman, the troupe's medico, reeled, staggering, holding his hands to his head; he was in charge of the juicing. Catching sight of the stooge, he stumbled toward him, nearly collapsing in his arms. The stooge caught him and held him up.

"Griffy!" Ullman shouted.

"What gives, Doc?!"

"Sabotage!"

"Wha—?"

"Sabotage, Griffy! Someone has tampered with the buffering solution!"

Ullman sprayed spittle from his foam-flecked lips.

"The buffer—someone switched it! I just checked the solution," he said. "It's not buffering agent, *it's Caterol!*"

"Huh? How could that happen?"

"I don't know, Griffy, I don't know! Someone must have gotten into the medicine chest and switched around the vials, replacing the buffer with full-strength Caterol!"

"Who'd do a crazy thing like that, Doc? And why?"

"I don't know, some business rivals of Mr. Calandria, perhaps—Griffy! Why are you looking at me like that? You don't think that I had something to do with this?!"

"Well, you're the doctor . . ."

"Don't even think it! It . . . it's monstrous to suggest that I'd be a party to such insanity! I know it looks bad, Griffy, but I'm completely innocent. You've got to believe me!"

"I believe you, Doc. Convincing the boss is going to be a tough sell, though."

Ullman's stricken face showed that he held a similar opinion. He sagged, holding onto Griffy for support. Griffy pried Ullman's clutching hands loose from his garments.

"You're wrinkling the material, Doc," he said, not ungently.

Ullman recoiled, lurching to one side. Somehow he managed to keep his footing and not fall. He was in bad shape.

Ten scheduled two-person matches added up to a total of twenty contestants. Twenty! All of them stoked and flying on drug-induced mindless kill-lust and temporarily endowed with superhuman strength. Overdosed, since the Caterol was undiluted by any buffers. Doubly overdosed, since the presumed buffering solution was really more Caterol, if Ullman was to be believed.

Those SCUs were sure taking a beating, but that's what they were made for. Nothing less than a bomb, burner, or beamer could make a dent in their tough plastex hides. The contestants couldn't even bring their crude weapons into play because they were locked into full body restraint until the hatches were unsealed. Their berserk struggling would succeed only in damaging themselves.

Who was behind it all? Rival promotors played rough but weren't suicidal, and that's what they would have to be to pull a gag like this on the boss.

Somebody had to tell the boss the bad news—but not Griffy. Who knew who he would lash out at with those horror tentacles in his first blind rage? Heads were going to roll for this; Ullman's, first, if he was lucky enough to get off that easily.

Time for Griffy to look after his own neck. *Better make sure Ullman doesn't get away . . .*

He looked for the medico, didn't see him at first, then noticed him heading for the exit. Griffy started after him, motioning to the door guards to intercept Ullman.

There was a thud, the sound of twenty SCUs simultaneously unsealing. They'd been sabotaged, too. Mag locks declamped, freeing bolts and deadfalls. Hatches popped open, releasing all restraints.

Twenty raging berserkers bristling with cutting and stabbing weapons leaped out of their upright coffins, ready to do battle, to kill, kill, *kill!*

Tony had just entered the arena, irked by the uproar but ignorant of its true nature. Crossing to the center of the ring, he raised his mek-arms high above his head, acknowledging the cheers of the crowd.

On cue, the overhead spotlights shone down into the cockpit, turning it into a well of white light. Bathed in radiance, mek-arms glinting like silver snakes, Tony waited for the noise to subside before making his little speech. A button-sized throat mike hooked up to a public address system and would effortlessly project his words to the uppermost tiers.

He opened his mouth to speak. Then shit things happened:

The SCUs opened, disgorging their occupants.

Outside, a series of explosions detonated as the luxury vehicles in the VIP parking area were blown to bits.

Indoors, lights flashed, flickered, strobed.

The curtain fell, exposing the backstage area to the audience.

Howling like banshees, lusting to destroy anything that lived, or even moved, the berserkers ran amok, hewing, hacking, ripping, rending.

Crew members ran for their lives. A few of the more steadfast guards managed to get off a shot or two before being torn apart limb from limb.

After a pause, the stupefied spectators reacted, stampeding for the exits. Scores were trampled, crushed to death.

Caterol-crazed amokers threw themselves into the throng, wreaking havoc. It was like tossing starving wolverines into a mass of lemmings.

A string of suspended glo-globes changed colors, spun, whirled, then smashed themselves against the sides of the tank.

It looked like a good time to get out of the cockpit. Tony turned to leave, but the exit was blocked. Somehow during the chaos the sliding door had dropped, barring the way.

That was only a minor problem for Tony, thanks to the firepower in his mek-arms. He hated to destroy the door because it was his own personal property and those things cost money, but he supposed it was foolish to be cheap during a crisis like this. He stepped back from the door to avoid being hit by shrapnel when he demolished it.

A flicker of motion overhead made him look up. A cockfighter stood crouching on top of the arena wall, a female contestant in a razor-bladed concertina wire bodysuit. Her face was as close to a ravening wolf's as it was possible for a human's to be. She saw Tony at the same time that he saw her.

She hurled herself, shrieking, into the cockpit, diving headfirst at Tony. Each blade of concertina wire wrapping her leathery brown unitard could slice flesh and blood to ribbons.

Tony gave her both barrels of the burner tubes implanted in his mek-arms, firing the UV heat rays at full power. Fan-shaped blasts of twinned red hell came pouring out of the burner muzzles in the palms of his metal hands. The contestant took the full force of the blast above the waist, liquefying in a burst of gore.

Mek-arm claws tore into the partly melted corpse, battering it away from Tony. It fell to the floor a mek-arm's length away from him. He backpedaled, tripped, and fell against the curved wall opposite the door.

Pawing the floor, another contestant lowered his head and prepared to charge. Tony fired an explosive shell into the middle of him, knocking him backward with pile-driver force.

Damn! The situation was starting to get hairy. He didn't have many more bombshells left.

The juggernaut's lower jaw was gone and there was a crater in his chest the size of a serving platter, but he still sat up. He got to his feet, readying for another charge.

Tony shot him with a bombshell, and then he didn't have a head. The body fell but continued to thrash around.

Humming sounded overhead, the deep-toned buzzing of some giant mechanical bee.

A sky-cycle descended through the square atrium that had been rayed out of the tank's roof for ventilation purposes.

Two ultra-light aircraft had been routinely parked on the roof as a precaution against airborne attack.

Basically a stripped-down mini-copter, the sky cycle had a hydrogen-powered engine mounted behind the pilot's seat. The four-bladed rotor assembly was enclosed in a grilled housing, as was the smaller tail rotor. The fuselage measured less than ten feet from stem to stern; the aircraft weighed about eight hundred pounds, and most of that was taken up by the engine.

Sky cycles were fast and ultra-maneuverable but fluky, prone to overturning despite their gyroscopic stabilizers. Whoever was at the controls of the aircraft hovering in the tank was one hell of a pilot.

Buzzing around like a fly in a bottle, the sky cycle provided the last little touch necessary to push the scene into total chaos. Hovering a hundred feet above the arena floor, it began slowly to descend. When it was a third of the way down, it swerved and plunged to avoid a runaway glo-globe. It dropped so fast that Tony thought it was going to crash and instinctively raised his mek-arms over his head, as if to ward it off.

It slowed at fifty feet and drifted to a halt fifteen feet below that. The amokers were enraged that they couldn't get at this infuriating noisemaker. Everyone else redoubled their efforts to escape before the sky cycle came crashing down on their heads.

The pilot was a big man in a roustabout's jumpsuit, his features hidden by a duck-billed cap and a pair of goggles. Reaching over the side, he freed one end of a coiled line that was fastened to the underside of the landing carriage. The line came looping down into the cockpit, making Tony jump back to avoid being hit.

A sling harness was fastened to the end of the line, but Tony ignored it. To hell with going airborne, he'd take his chances on the ground! Only suddenly he didn't have a choice, because the noisy sky cycle was drawing all the amokers to it. From all corners, they made a beeline to it, and to the cockpit over which it hovered. It was out of their reach, but Tony wasn't.

Damning the idiot pilot who had endangered him by trying to rescue him, Tony fitted his arms through the sling and pulled it down over his head, making it snug across his chest and under his arms. The pilot was watching, and as soon as the sling was safely in place, he took off.

With a jerk and a pull, Tony's feet left the floor and he began his ascent. The cockpit's curved walls fell away from him. The top of it was ringed by berserkers who were catapulted into new paroxysms of rage by his escape. An axe was thrown at him, and missed. Hands grabbed for him, but he was out of their reach.

An amoker climbed up on the lip of the cockpit and flung himself at Tony. A mek-arm clubbed him aside, breaking his neck before he fell into the cockpit. He got up, head lolling at a grotesque angle, vainly grasping at empty air.

Tony was now high enough to break his own neck should he fall. As if responding to his worry, the sky cycle took a sudden lurch. Tony grabbed for the line with both hands, then checked himself. If he grabbed too tightly, his hydraulic-powered metal-fingered grip was likely to sever the line like scissors snipping string. He closed his fists on the line very carefully, vowing to promote the pilot for saving him and then pulverize him for risking his skin in the first place.

The floor fell away; the roof rushed toward him. The atrium hole didn't look very big. Tony closed his eyes as the sky cycle neared it. Then it was through and still rising, hauling him up at the end of a forty-foot line.

Night air buffeted him. Tony opened his eyes and looked down. Bodies lay sprawled on top of the tank, the bodies of the sentries who had been posted there. But if they were dead, who was piloting the sky cycle?

In the time it had taken to formulate that thought, the aircraft had climbed another hundred feet.

The seriousness of Tony's predicament sank in on him. He still had enough ammo left in the mek-arms to kill the pilot and wreck the sky cycle, but all that would buy him was a two-hundred-foot drop straight down. Three hundred feet now, for the sky cycle kept steadily rising.

The holocaust of burning, wrecked cars below, which must have been blown up simply as a diversion, now looked as small as a camp fire. The sky was dark, and the great black earth rushed away from Tony in all directions.

Four-hundred feet now, five-hundred, six-hundred—

Humming sounded overhead, not the mechanical buzzing of the fanlike rotor blades, but a deep vibratory drone, the sound of great power under harness somewhere in the sky.

A dark cigar-shaped object, darker than the darkness, hung motionless above the sky cycle. Here was the source of the mysterious sound. The sky cycle rose to meet it.

The unknown aircraft was torpedo-shaped, about thirty feet long, wingless except for small stabilizing tailfins. Its running lights were dark, a clear violation of aviation law, branding it as an outlaw bird, but no outlaws Tony had ever heard of piloted an aircraft like it.

Slowing to a speed of a few miles an hour, the sky cycle drifted upward toward the underside of the aircraft. They were on a collision course. They were going to crash!

Tony screamed, a thin, bleating wail that was lost in the immensity surrounding him. The sky cycle touched the ship as softly as a kiss, guided into place by a magnetic docking baffle grid located amidships. The top side of the rotor cage housing locked onto the docking grid as securely as if it had been welded there.

The pilot leaned over the side, pointed a hand weapon at Tony, and fired. A stream of shock charges peppered Tony, outlining him in harsh blue light. They overrode the mek-arms' weakened defenses, shorting them out. He smelled hot metal, burned wiring, ozone. Then his brain shorted out, too, and he ceased to know anything at all.

When he awoke, he was in the cage on the barge, floating down the main drag of Beamer Junction toward the substation. He was literally disarmed, his mechanical prosthetics having been removed from the flipperlike appendages protruding from his shoulders. Around the torso he had been chained to the bars in a sitting-up position, to keep him from falling over . . .

• • •

Enro Blugeld had been snatched in broad daylight. He was a much-feared action agent for Bill Braun's GodSword, a deep-pocketed extremist organization that served as an umbrella for a variety of lesser hate groups, supplying them with aid and comfort: political terrorism, arson, bombings, torture, and murder. Blugeld had honchoed the birth of death squads operated by like-minded law enforcement personnel in over a dozen different cities in East and South Central Texas and Louisiana. He was currently on assignment in Rubric, a wealthy suburb outside Middletown.

Blugeld was in church, even though it was a weekday afternoon. He was there to rehearse his part in a little presentation ceremony scheduled to follow next Sunday's services. He was going to be thanked by the chairman of the board of trustees for making a big contribution to the church's coffers. The donation had been made from GodSword funds, but if the trustees knew, they didn't care, as long as the real source of the money didn't become common knowledge. Politics, that's what it was. Bill Braun was very big on building bridges to establishment figures: churchmen, politicians, police brass, and business leaders. Unlike many of the party's rowdier elements, Blugeld was smooth enough to function in polite society. Lately the party's general staff had been easing him out of action operations and into more high-profile politicking. Blugeld was happy to have the change. Action ops were getting chancier; the victims were starting to fight back. He'd been out in the field long enough and now welcomed the gravy jobs.

His part in the planned ceremony was minimal. All he had to do was step up to the podium to accept a certificate of commendation from the chairman, who would present it on behalf of the entire congregation. It was understood that he'd say a few words of thanks for the honor, as few and as generalized as possible, with no political commentary. Basically his part was a walk-through, but he'd come by this afternoon to learn his entrances and exits, and to give his security staff a look-see so they could plan their arrangements for Sunday.

Blugeld was thick-featured, coarsely handsome, big-armed, and deep-chested. His personal style was subdued, tasteful, with only three earrings piercing his left ear—the minimum allowed by fashion—and short-hair dyed uniformly in one color, platinum blond. Blue contact lenses protected his eyes from solar flares, beamer and burner glare, and hypno rays. Anti-hypno safeguards were an obsession with Bill Braun, who was in dread of having the security of his inner circle penetrated by mind-bending enemy agents. Shunning uniforms, epaulets, ribbons, arm bands, and other badges of authority that his high rank entitled him to, Blugeld dressed in the same style of expensively subdued garments worn by the leaders of the community. A button-sized lapel pin bearing the flaming sword insignia of the party was his sole outward symbol of affiliation with GodSword.

Lethal weapons of great destructive power were concealed on his person, but he wore no guns. To go about openly armed in Texas was understood to mean that the wearer subscribed to the unwritten conventions of the Code Duello. One of these articles of faith was the right of an offended party to seek a redress of grievances by challenging the offender to a duel of honor. Declining a legitimate duel was a social stigma in some circles, leading to serious loss of face. Blugeld went without a sidearm to avoid being challenged by those who had suffered because of the party, should any of them somehow get through his screen of security staffers.

Synthesized organ music churned through the speakers in the high-ceilinged church, filling it with a solemn Gothic dirge. Synthesist and choir performed behind gauzy curtains enclosing a space in the wall behind and fifteen feet above the altar. The choir was absent today, but the synthesist had come in to provide the musical cues at the rehearsal.

Parson Clark and trustees Nimrod and Oldfield stood chatting with Blugeld at the foot of the altar steps. The trustees were Blugeld's men on the board and had helped persuade the chairman to agree to the ceremony of commendation. Bribery had clinched the argument. Parson Clark remained willfully oblivious to board politics.

The music was loud, and they had to raise their voices to be heard over it.

"Is that the music that's going to be played on Sunday when I get the award?"

"Goodness, no, Brother Blugeld," Parson Clark said.

"Good. You had me worried there for a minute. It sounds like funeral music. I'm here to get a scroll of thanks, not the last rites. Not that it's not a deeply moving piece, Parson."

"It is inspirational, is it not? Odd, I've never heard Nichols play it before . . . He certainly is doing a masterful job of it, though."

"I could go for something a little more up-tempo myself," Oldfield said.

"Yes, hadn't we better get on with the rehearsal, Parson? We're all busy men here and time is precious," Nimrod said.

"Indeed. Nichols can resume practicing when we're done. Still it seems almost a sin to interrupt him when he's playing so beautifully. Confidentially, I wish he played this well at Sunday services. I've never heard him play with such a sure touch," Parson Clark said.

He glanced upward at the curtained sound pit from which the music came.

High above them, Mickey Hruska was the first to see the airship. One of Blugeld's security staff, he was in the belfry of the church spire making an inspection tour when the attack came.

The octagonal belfry was crowned by a needle-like spire fifty feet tall. A radar mini-antenna rotated on a gimbal at the point of the apex, scanning the skies over Rubric—yellow sky, bleached blue-white where it met the circle of the horizon.

No bells in the belfry, of course, just four horn-shaped speakers mounted on a metal stand, connected to audio equipment that played the sound of chimes through them as needed. Clear polycarbonate shields covering the tower's eight archways were retracted for the ringing of the "bells," then lowered into place at the completion of the tolling.

Coolpoint suit or not, Mickey couldn't take the mid-afternoon heat in the tower. He felt like he was going to puke. He pressed the button that rolled up the shields, letting in the outside air. It provided little relief, and he still felt like he was going to puke, even more than before. Pressing his palms against the waist-high sill of the archway opening out over the front of the church, he leaned forward and stuck his head out. If he got sick, he'd do it on the gabled roof instead of in the belfry.

When he stuck his head outside the protection in the tower, the naked sunlight struck him like a hammer.

That's when he saw the ship.

Automatic alarm machinery monitoring the detectors switched on, red lights flashing, needles sweeping across gauges, buzzers sounding. But the burst of activity ended as suddenly as it had begun. Red lights dimmed, needles whipsawed from one end of the gauges to the other, buzzers squawked and fell silent, viewscreens were filled with "snow."

A heartbeat later, the cycle repeated itself. The machinery activated as if responding to an intruder, then just as suddenly switched off as if the intruder weren't really there.

The cycle repeated again and again, as if somehow the machinery couldn't make up its mind. Mickey would have thought that the hardware was on the blink, if not for the airship.

It came in low, below the tops of the buildings lining both sides of the avenue leading to the front of the church. Blunt-nosed and cigar-shaped, with stubby tailfins, it looked like some metal shark of the skies.

What was important was what didn't happen. Like all structures called upon at one time or another to house important people, the church was protected against airborne attack. When the unknown aircraft first appeared on the detector screens, the air defense system should have automatically armed the battery of antiaircraft missiles in the spire, then launched them as soon as the intruder had failed to respond to a questing probe-beam with the proper identification code signal.

That's what should have happened. Instead, the ADS was going berserk, its computer logic deranged, unable to decide if the aircraft was there or wasn't.

Mickey knew better; he could see the damned thing coming straight at him. It was closing the distance fast, too. His job required him to keep abreast of the latest developments in weaponry, so he had a pretty good idea of what the intruder was: a subzee cruiser, better armed than a scout boat and faster and more maneuverable than a gunship. Cruisers were rare, with most of the models still in the developmental stage, years from general release, even to those few who could afford such expensive, ultra-sophisticated aircraft. GodSword didn't have any.

The cruiser had to be protected with some kind of cloaking device to thwart the ADS detectors. That's what was giving the automatic target recognition system fits. Mickey lunged for the manual override switch on the device. He could cut the ATR out of the circuit and launch the antiaircraft missiles at the intruder.

The cruiser acted first, firing a salvo of thermal flares to one side of the spire. Mickey hit the override switch, but he was too late. Relays snapped into place as the ADS detectors automatically responded to the hot infrared signature of the flares.

The flares were bright white-hot streaks of incandescence. Hatches popped open in the spire as a battery of AAMs ignited and launched to intercept what their deceived sensors told them was an enemy aircraft. The belfry shook from the vibrations of the multiple blast-off.

The AAMs tore through the flare zone and kept on going, arcing high on an irreversible trajectory to nowhere. By accident or design the flares had been targeted for a quadrant of sky to ensure that the misguided missiles would eventually crash in empty landscape rather than in a populated area. That was scant consolation to Mickey and the rest of Blugeld's bodyguards as they scrambled to counter the oncoming threat.

Shooting erupted down below, on the ground in front of the church, as a half-dozen bodyguards hauled out their hardware and started blasting at the cruiser. Mickey grabbed his mini-machine gun and opened up at the aircraft, which was now only a traffic square away.

A chain gun in the cruiser's nose returned fire, strafing the bodyguards on the ground with a stream of .50-caliber bullets that ripped them up and laid them out.

Too late Mickey knew that the cruiser's armaments operated on auto-defense, shooting back only at what had shot at them first. He never felt the chain-gun burst that sieved him and the belfry.

Inside the church, Blugeld reacted at the first sound of gunfire. Holding his arms well out from his sides, he gave them an unnatural reverse-twist, activating twin spring-sleeve holsters. A pair of gun butts smacked against his waiting palms, filling his hands with a burner and a four-barreled mini-missile launcher.

"Good heavens!" Parson Clark said.

Cullinane and Darden, Blugeld's two best guns, were never far from him. Cullinane was in the second-floor balcony on the east wall of the church; Darden was at the opposite end of the nave from the altar, between the closed front doors and the last row of the pews. They had their guns out, too, but there was nothing to shoot at yet.

The funereal music kept on playing, as if nothing were happening, the synthesizer keyboardist not missing a note.

Blugeld and company faced the front of the church, where the shooting was coming from. The parson shuddered in synchronization with the bursts of chain-gun firing.

A shadow appeared on the magnificent stained glass window above the front doors, a circular mosaic some thirty feet in diameter that depicted Christ scourging the money changers from the temple.

At first no bigger than a man's hand, the shadow grew and darkened, spreading like an ink blot until at last it covered almost all of the multicolored window.

Then the mosaic imploded, disintegrating into a hail of rainbow shards falling inside the church. The cruiser plowed through the window frame at a speed of a few miles per hour, and hung suspended in midair. Its hum of power vibrated like the keening of a celestial choir.

There was other music, too, the continuing dirge of the synthesized funeral march thundering toward its climax. The import of that clicked inside Cullinane's head; he pivoted, swinging his gun barrel toward the choir pit above the altar.

From that direction came a bombshell round that tagged him dead-on center, catapulting his ragged corpse halfway across the church.

Darden and Nimrod were firing at the cruiser, their slugs flattening into leaden smears against the aircraft's bullet-proof composite armor. They were not so immune to the cruiser's return fire, which cut them down.

Crouching between the pews, Blugeld was glad that he had held his fire. The four explosive warheads tipping the mini-missiles in his hand-held launcher might take down the cruiser, but if they didn't, its guns would surely get him.

Gauzy curtains parted, fluttering as a figure bulled through them to the lip of the choir pit. The figure wore white choir robes and a battle helmet with the visor down, hiding its face.

Oldfield shouted something unintelligible while firing a burst at the newcomer. He missed, punching a line of craters into the wall. The newcomer ducked, rolled to one side, stopped, and squeezed off a shot from the prone position, nailing Oldfield. Oldfield flipped backward, head over heels.

Chancing that the cruiser's auto-defense wouldn't target him as long as he didn't shoot at it, Blugeld popped up and cut loose with two mini-missiles.

But the stranger had already jumped down from the choir pit, dropping nimbly to the altar before the minis struck, filling the space he had just quitted with explosive hellfire.

He hit the floor rolling, tumbling across the altar, firing a shot before diving off the edge of the raised platform.

A shock charge hit Blugeld, unleashing its energy in a sizzling blue bolt. He was instantly paralyzed, muscles knotting into iron hardness, heart squeezed by an invisible fist of electricity. The charge shorted out his anti-shock defenses, the only thing keeping him conscious.

Blugeld fell backward into a cushioned pew. The charge's effect negated all the victim's volitional muscle activity, while leaving untouched the body's autonomic processes. He couldn't move, couldn't even blink, but his heart and lungs kept working, keeping him alive. Other types of shock charges weren't so merciful.

The funeral music had stopped, silenced when the explosions destroyed the prerecorded music crystal the stranger had loaded into the playback system, to counterfeit the sound of a live synthesist. Cullinane had guessed the trick but too late.

"Parson Clark," the stranger said, his voice emanating from the extro-speakers mounted on his helmet.

Parson Clark remained where he was, facedown, hugging the floor.

"No sense playing possum, preacher man, I know you can hear me. You better lay low for a while longer in case there's any more shooting. Blugeld's boys aren't too particular about who they burn down, in case you hadn't heard," the stranger said.

Debris crunched under his booted feet as he made his way toward the parson.

"Just wanted to let you know that you'll find the real Nichols locked in the closet in the chancery office. I gave him a light charge which should wear off soon," he said.

Daring to look up, the parson raised his plaster-dusted face from the floor. The stranger was a big man, well-armed, wearing an outfit that looked like a cross between a flight suit and a scaled flexi-armor bodysuit.

Plucking Blugeld's weapons from his hands and tossing them aside, he said, "I know you can hear me so let's do it right. Enro Maurice Blugeld, I arrest you for conspiracy to commit murder, which is contrary to the laws of the state of Texas, you skunk."

Bending forward from the waist, he hoisted Blugeld to his feet and slung him across his shoulder like a sack of dirty laundry. Blugeld weighed 225 pounds, but the stranger wasn't even straining.

He punched in a series of numbers on the keypad inside of his left forearm guard. Responding to the coded instructions, the cruiser drifted downward, arresting its descent a few feet above the floor of the nave. Another, shorter coded sequence caused the cruiser to lower a fold-out stepladder on the port side, beneath the cockpit.

With Blugeld in tow, the stranger climbed the stepladder. The teardrop-shaped canopy slid back, opening the cockpit. Reaching inside, he pressed a hidden stud, which unlatched a square-shaped compartment behind the cockpit. He dumped Blugeld into it, dropping him so that he landed on his head. Closing the hatch, he stripped off the choir robe, saying, "Thanks for the loan," as he cast it aside. He climbed into the cockpit and sat down, the chair's safety harness automatically snugging around him.

"You'll have to hold a heap of bake sales to pay for building repairs, Preacher. Why not ask Bill Braun for another donation?"

"You—you've wrecked my church, you madman! *Who are you?!*"

"The Lord moves in mysterious ways, Parson. I'm one of them," the stranger said.

The stepladder folded into its niche and the canopy began to slide shut.

"Don't forget to duck," the stranger added before the canopy closed.

Shots and shouts came from outside. Blugeld's reinforcements were arriving. That was one of GodSword's strengths, patrol units roving citywide that were able to respond to emergencies at short notice. This wasn't the kind of emergency they were used to responding to, though.

The keening drone of the cruiser's engines deepened, and lifting six feet above the floor, it floated in reverse toward the front of the church.

A rear-mounted pocket rocket flamed on, lancing toward the tall peaked front doors, disintegrating them in a blast.

The concussion caught some of Blugeld's men who were racing up the stone front steps, scattering them like bowling pins. One of them jerked the trigger of a shoulder-mounted beam tube launcher as he was flung into the air. A bolt of jagged blue lightning leaped from the tube, spearing through roiling smoke to strike the spire by mistake. A thunderclap boomed as the short-lived blast of manmade lightning pulverized the base of the tower, toppling it.

The cruiser glided through the jagged, still-smoking entryway where the doors used to be, continuing to fly backward. Some of those who had been on the fringes of the blast area fired at the cruiser, only to be mowed down an instant later by side-mounted auto-defense guns.

Two patrol units were racing toward the church, closing in on it. A pickup truck with a recoilless rifle mounted on the bed of the hopper raced down the main avenue, while a six-wheeled land van packed with a goon squad of a dozen party bullyboys came careening in from a side street.

Pointing its tail at the oncoming gun truck, the cruiser shot backward toward it on a collision course. Its underside skimmed the street with a scant twelve inches of clearance between it and the blacktop, coming in so low that the gun truck couldn't drop its mini-cannon low enough to train the muzzle on it.

Wrestling the steering wheel hard over to one side in a frantic effort to avoid a crash, the driver lost control. The gun truck tipped, both tires on one side leaving the ground. It overturned and rolled, spraying sparks, mashing metal, and pulping its flesh-and-blood occupants.

Without warning, the cruiser shot straight up in the air, smoothly translating its reverse motion into a vertical climb. Soaring like a runaway balloon, it dwindled in the distant heights.

The six-wheeler screeched to a halt in the traffic square, disgorging a dozen gunmen from its rear hatch. They were equipped with lightweight body armor, anti-shock insulated boots, half-helmets with comm links, assault rifles, grenades, and sidearms. Deploying into three-man teams, they took cover and prepared to do battle.

Rubric's police force kept their distance from the scene, following departmental policy to steer clear of GodSword business.

After a moment, the squadsmen realized that the fight was over. Emerging from cover, they converged in the center of the square around the van, heads tilted backward as they tried to see the cruiser, which had dwindled to a speck high above them.

"Now what do we do?" one of them said.

The distant speck suddenly grew larger as it plummeted toward them, swooping down out of the sky.

"Here it comes again! Run, *run!*"

A few shouldered their rifles and started firing, but the majority turned tail and scrambled for cover. The cruiser's shadow fell on the square, swelling as the aircraft came in on a steep dive.

The chain gun opened up, chopping the riflemen who stayed to fight. A pair of pocket rockets flung themselves free from the cruiser and leaped ahead of it, fast widening the gap between them and it, outracing it to the square. Trailing thin vapor trails, they homed in on the six-wheeler's hot engine, slamming into it and blowing the van to bits. Flaming debris rained down for a city block.

The cruiser pulled up out of the dive at the last instant, winds shrieking across its streamlined surfaces as it nosed up and leveled off. It flew so low that the airstream of its passage tore unfastened helmets off heads and sucked a trail of debris in its wake.

It climbed to an altitude of a thousand feet, veered to the southwest, and then was gone.

One of the squadsmen voiced the question that was uppermost in all the survivors' minds:

"How're we going to explain this to Bill?"

Doc Endocrine went to the receiving area to personally inspect the latest shipment of spare parts.

"Hollister and McKay's last shipment was definitely unsatisfactory," he said, thin lips pursed in prim distaste.

"What are you gonna do, Doc? They can't all be winners,"

"They'd better be, at the prices we're paying, Fulton."

Fulton was the orderly in charge of reception, a blue-jawed thug in a soiled white doctor's tunic that bulged at his right hip where his sidearm was holstered. He was a squat strongman who'd worked in snake-pit mental hospitals, horror house nursing homes, and similar institutions. An unsavory individual at best, thought the doctor, but necessary for dealing with the likes of Hollister and McKay.

"You shouldn't have accepted that last consignment, Fulton."

"Aw, Hollister and McKay almost always come through with the straight goods. Everybody's entitled to a clunker once in a while."

"You're very generous with my money."

"Consider it a public relations expense to build a little goodwill with the suppliers, Doc. You don't want to get on the wrong side of those two ghouls. Otherwise, your carcass is liable to turn up on a slab at one of the competition's clinics."

"You overestimate them. They're merely a pair of very ordinary hoodlums."

"Maybe so, maybe so. But it ain't you who'd have to face them and tell them that they weren't going to get paid for the delivery."

"Our clients pay an obscene amount of money for our services here at the clinic, Fulton. They expect and demand first-class working organs from disease-free donors. The donors from the last shipment were just so much worthless trash, Skid Row gutter sweepings at their last extremity. Hardly a viable kidney or liver in the lot."

"Like you didn't use them anyway."

"That's not the point, Fulton. It's the principle of the thing. I refuse to pay top dollar for damaged goods."

"They tossed in a few clunkers to make quota. So what? They'll make up for it this time or next. Even ghouls have to make a living, Doc."

"How much of the fee did they kick back to you, Fulton?"

"Now, now, Doc, I've got to make a living, too. Besides which, you don't pay me enough to cross Hollister and McKay."

"I'm not afraid of them."

"No? You'll get a chance to prove it. They're due any minute now."

"That's why I'm here."

"Remind me to keep out of the line of fire, Doc. If anything happens to you, at least I know where to send the body. Right here," Fulton said, meaning the clinic.

The clandestine clinic. This was a black medicine body shop and Doc Endocrine was a secret "Frankenscientist," the slang word to describe the crime doctors who trafficked in forbidden medical practices. Unauthorized organ transplants, brainwashes and mind wipes, glandular reenergizers, prohibited cybernetic implants, poison vending, the synthesis of Ferol and its derivatives (including Caterol) . . . these were only a few of the many biochemical crimes lumped under the label of "black medicine."

Publicly, in his persona of Doc Endocrine, Dr. Horace Enright was the founder and figurehead of Doc Endocrine's All-Natural Glandular Extracts, a line of pills and potions widely sold in health food centers in South Texas. Claiming to promote good health and virility in its users, the main ingredient of the products was compounded of glandular secretions extracted from domestic animals, particularly sheep, goats, cattle, and primates. The trade was strictly legal, although every now and then militant animal rights extremists managed to hijack one of the doctor's trucks and blow it up, or maim an employee by raying him off below the knees. But that was okay; the doctor had insurance to cover such mishaps.

Although the extract-vending did manage to turn a tidy profit, it was only a cover for an incredibly lucrative and ultra-illegal covert body shop clinic he had been running for some years. It was hidden under a warehouse in the waterfront district of the bustling river port of Trident, where three rivers came together some sixty miles south of San Antonio. If the citizens ever found out what Doc

Endocrine was really up to, they'd tear him limb from limb, but there was little chance of that. He was protected by the syndicate, a working alliance between the local branches of the Texas mob and the Mexicrime cartel. A crooked doctor was a useful asset. Such was the logic of Trident's police higher-ups, too, who did their part to see that the Frankenscientist wasn't interfered with.

Which was one reason why the medico wasn't afraid of Hollister and McKay. They knew that their hides wouldn't be worth spit if they harmed him. And just in case they forgot their good sense, a UV burner disguised as a physician's mirror would remind them. The round mirror-backed light, attached to an insulated headband and worn in the middle of Doc Endocrine's forehead, seemed nothing more than an ordinary medical instrument, but in a fraction of a second it could ray a hole as wide as a pencil through a man's brain at a distance of ten paces. Fulton didn't know about it, either.

A buzzer sounded, and a light flashed on the instrument panel of the security monitoring system.

"That must be them," Fulton said.

Going to the work station, he flipped switches and turned dials, activating the closed-circuit spy-eye camera mounted over the bay door that fronted a black river. Fifty years earlier, the watercourse had barely been an anemic trickle, little more than an overgrown stream, but the changing weather patterns of the post–Greenhouse effect climate had put the once-arid region squarely in the Gulf storm belt, swelling its waterways into great surging rivers. The unpredictable nature of the region's meteorological trends was demonstrated by the fact that desert-dry Badlands lay only a few score miles west of the Tres Rios district.

With its lights off, an ambulance idled on the tarmac bordering the bay door. It was a wheeled vehicle powered by a standard hydrogen-fueled engine, equipped with auxiliary turbo-fans capable of short-term hovercraft capacity for traversing short stretches of rugged terrain and bodies of water. The hovercraft option was very useful for evading pursuit. Originally colored antiseptic white, the ambulance had been begrimed to a dingy gray. Layers of dirt filmed the red and gold logos on its sides, the twin snake-and-staff logo associated with physicians since the days of Hippocrates. Inscribed above the emblems were the words "JIFFY AMBULANCE SERVICE When Speed is of the Essence."

Jiffy was a freelance ambulance service. Day and night its mobile units cruised the city, monitoring police and hospital radio frequencies for reported fires, shootings, traffic accidents, and other disasters. There was no shortage of life-threatening catastrophes in Trident, especially not on the bustling docks and in the rowdy waterfront dives. On receipt of an emergency call, independent ambulances would race to the scene, frequently causing other accidents in their haste to be the first to arrive at the disaster site. Brawls and even gunfights could result when rival services clashed over who got to carry away the injured.

The paramedic crews would load the injured on stretchers, throw them in the ambulances, and rush them to the emergency room of the nearest hospital. En route, the casualties' Universal credit card numbers would be punched into the onboard billing system, transferring the amount of the delivery fee to the service's account via electronic banking. Hard currency was acceptable for payment, as were gems, precious metals, holographic crystals, drugs, weapons, and other valuables. Passengers with bad or no credit ratings and nothing to barter were unceremoniously dumped on the nearest street corner, often while the vehicle was still moving. The freelance ambulance game was a tough competitive business with no time to waste in carting deadbeats.

As for the more criminally minded ambulance crews, the body shops were always on the lookout for new organ "donors." They paid in cash with no questions asked. Such a crew was the team of Hollister and McKay, prowling the city streets from dusk to dawn. The night dispatcher at Jiffy knew about the racket but kept his mouth shut in return for a share of the take. When business was slow, the duo would rig accidents or start fires to up the body count. They'd been known to snatch healthy people off the street to make their quota. Their arrangement with Doc Endocrine gave him first choice of the nightly harvest.

The spy-eye's night-vision lens showed the scene outside the bay door with hard-edged clarity on the monitor viewscreens. McKay was in the operator's cab; Hollister must have been in the ambulance, overseeing the "patients," making sure that they were drugged into insensibility. The fresher the donor, the more successful the transplant; live donors were the freshest of all.

Visual identification alone was not enough to gain admittance to the clinic. Those seeking entry also had to transmit the proper recognition code signal, which was changed weekly. This precaution was taken not in fear of a police raid—there was little fear of that, since the fix was in—but rather to deter raids from rival clinics.

McKay keyed in the correct code. The bay's sliding door rolled up and the ambulance rolled in, its parking lights casting a ghostly glow in the dim, cavernous interior. The door rolled down and closed.

Neon green lightstrips came on, outlining a square section of floor measuring ten feet on a side. The ambulance parked in the outlined area. From below came the muffled throb of machinery.

The floor seemed to rise as the ten-foot square slowly fell away from it. It was the platform of a disguised freight elevator. It lowered the ambulance into an underground chamber, coming to rest with a soft bump.

Tube lights filled the space with cool, cheerless brightness. The underground garage had stone walls and floor and a metal ceiling. The stone was steel-reinforced concrete, a crude but effective building material that had long been superseded by the modern poured ferrocrete technique in A.D. 2035. The underground rooms were ancient, possibly as much as a century old, and must have existed long before the warehouse was built, since its ceiling—the warehouse's main floor—was made of ferrocrete slabs reinforced by metalloy beams and girders.

A pair of horizontal sliding panels opened in a wall, accessing the receiving area, a slightly larger room with a ramp and loading platform adjacent to the clinic proper. The driver backed the rear of the ambulance to the bottom of the ramp and switched off the motor. He got out and went around to the rear of the vehicle.

Fulton came down to meet him. "How's tricks, Mac?" he said.

McKay shrugged. His sallow, raw-boned face was stiff, immobile. Only the eyes were alive in that dead visage. They were sharp, shrewd, watchful. A duck-billed cap was pulled down on his head; the hair beneath it was a coarse black mop. He wore hospital whites, a long-sleeved tunic and baggy pants, and he stood slouching, with shoulders hunched and his chin resting on his chest.

Fulton guided a triple-tiered suspensor gurney to the back of the ambulance. Glancing at the open doorway to the examining room to make sure that his boss wasn't around, he said, low-voiced, "Doc's attitudey tonight, Mac. He's pissed about those rumdums in your last shipment."

McKay grunted, shrugged.

"Weeeeeell, I just hope you've got something good for him tonight to make up for last time."

"It's good," McKay said.

He spoke in a husky near-whisper, hardly moving his mouth, a mode of speech often found in those who have spent time in prison, where frequently talking is forbidden to the inmates.

"I stuck my neck way out when I okayed that last batch. You stuck me with some real clunkers," Fulton said.

McKay didn't say anything, just looked at him until Fulton looked away.

"Better get the show on the road. The doc's waiting," Fulton said at last.

He turned the handle of the ambulance's rear hatch, unsealing it.

"Hollister in back?" he said.

"Uh-huh."

Fulton rolled back the hatch and climbed into the stuffy, poorly lit compartment. Antiseptic deodorizers fought and lost with the stench of blood and voided bodily wastes. A row of dim ceiling-mounted glo-discs filled the space with murky yellow-brown light. The middle aisle was flanked by double-tiered racks, each rack able to hold four adult bodies. They were empty, except for a pair of bodies laid out side by side on the bottom tier of the right side. Stained sheets shrouded the corpses.

"Only two? Doc's going to be disappointed. Must have been a slow night, huh?"

"It's not over yet," McKay said from behind him.

"Hey, I thought you said Hollister was in here."

"He is."

"I don't see him—"

"Look harder."

McKay chuckled, sending chills along Fulton's spine. The truth dawned on Fulton as he stood staring at the sheeted bodies.

"You mean—"

Fulton broke off, choking, gorge rising. Swallowing hard, he fought down his nausea.

"B-But Hollister was your partner!"

"Business is business."

"I don't believe it. You two have been partners for years! This is some kind of gag, right?"

"See for yourself," McKay said.

With trembling hands, Fulton reached for the shroud and turned it down, uncovering the corpses above the neck. They lay on their backs, faceup, unlovely in death, their sightless eyes filmed over.

Hollister—and McKay.

His head swimming, Fulton clutched an upper-tier strut for support to keep from being floored by the shock.

"*McKay*—?! But if that's McKay, then who—*Urk!!*"

The Donor Processing Center was half-autopsy room, half-slaughterhouse—a big room with green-tiled walls, a rubber-matted floor, and metalloy sinks, fixtures, and operating tables. Tables (equipped with grooves and drains), life-support equipment, oxygen tanks, instrument trays, medicine chests, autoclave sterilizers, and storage bins crowded for space. Most of one of the smaller walls was taken up by the insulated metalloy door of a walk-in freezer. Ventilation ducts kept the air circulating; the chill coming off the freezer held the room temperature to a brisk 65 degrees.

A drum-shaped cool-light glo-globe hung from the ceiling above the operating tables in the center of the room. Grouped around a centrally located vital signs monitoring console were Doc Endocrine, Dr. Vansittart, his assistant, and Hugo, the surgical technician who actually did the cutting, sawing, and chopping. All three wore sterile surgical caps, gowns, and latex gloves.

"Go see what the delay is, Hugo—Oh, never mind, here's McKay now," Doc Endocrine said.

Holding it by the handlebar, McKay guided the suspensor gurney to the operating tables, its simple magnetic lifters holding its flat bottom several inches above the floor, riding on a cushion of invisible force.

It held three shrouded bodies stacked vertically, one on each tier.

"Where's Fulton?"

"He's around, Doc."

"I've got a bone to pick with you and your partner, McKay. That last shipment you brought me was a disgrace, an absolute disgrace! What few organs I could salvage from the mess had a rejection rate of 73 percent, and that's giving them the benefit of the doubt."

The gurney bumped against one of the tables. The soft impact was enough to dislodge the hands of the corpse on the upper tier. An arm flopped down over the edge, dragging part of the shroud with it, baring the cadaver's face.

It was Fulton. His head lolled at a crazy angle and ugly purple-black bruises marked where strong hands had taken hold of his neck and snapped it.

"Oops," McKay said.

Doc Endocrine thrust his head forward and scrunched up his forehead, a preprogrammed sequence of movements that activated the burner concealed in his round mirror. A thin ray of ruby-red laser light ripped through the space were McKay's head had been a split-second before. The ray burned a hole six inches deep and a half-inch wide in the opposite wall.

McKay had ducked down behind the gurney. Doc Endocrine turned his head toward him, swinging the red ray into line. Sizzling through the air, it struck the gurney's polished metalloy surface and was deflected, splintering into a sunburst of ruby shafts.

Dr. Vansittart and Hugo dove for cover.

McKay hooked his hands under the bottom of the gurney and lifted, straightening his legs as he did so. Muscles flexed and joints popped. The gurney tilted to one side, spilling the corpses from their tiers.

They crashed into Doc Endocrine, tangling him up, knocking him down. He fell on his back, pinned under dead men. He hit the back of his head against the floor and saw stars.

The ray kept on burning, a thin red vertical line of light boring into the ceiling. The medico smoothed out his forehead, but the burner refused to switch off as it should have. It kept on working at full power. Its power cell, a micro-chip the size of a pinhead, was unable to sustain the load for more than a minute. The ray darkened and grew fuzzier as the cell overheated.

A pinpoint of warmth appeared on Doc Endocrine's forehead where the cell was located. Within seconds the tingling warm spot became as hot as the tip of a soldering iron. Roaring with pain, he tore off the headband and flung it as far away as he could.

There was a tremendous crash as the overturned gurney fell on its side, the magnetic lifters having automatically shut off when it dropped below a 45-degree angle.

McKay popped up from behind a table. Hugo grabbed a hand-held bone cutter and went after him. The instrument was shaped something like a flashlight, except that the business end of it was a high-speed rotary mini-buzzsaw that cut bone like scissors cut paper.

Hugo lunged, striking downward with a vicious overhand slash. McKay sidestepped out of its path. Hugo, carried off-balance by the momentum of his swing, tried to recover.

McKay grabbed Hugo's wrist, pulling him forward so he stumbled. He turned the wrist, doubling the hand and the bone cutter back toward Hugo and thrusting the saw into his chest.

A stranger stepped into view, beamer in hand. His black wig was askew. His face was a tiger-striped pattern formed of the tattered remains of the McKay mask and his own face showing beneath it. He was blood-spattered from his impromptu surgery on Hugo. The tip of his beamer muzzle glowed dull red.

To Doc Endocrine, he looked like an avenging demon from some bloody pit of Hell.

The medico could figure out what had happened easily enough. The stranger had gotten the drop on Hollister and McKay and gotten the secret recognition code from them before killing them. Then he used a blank mask to counterfeit a replica of McKay's face, probably molding it directly from the original, a true death mask. That was the how of it. The why and most especially the who of it were mysteries to the doctor.

"I don't know you," he said. "Who are you?"

"I'm the Man."

"What man?"

"The man that's putting you out of business, Doc."

A tongue of lightning burst from the beamer and licked Doc Endocrine on the chest, sending him crashing into oblivion.

The beamer must have been set to stun, not kill, for the doctor awoke to find himself back in the land of the living. He was chained to the bars of a cage on a floating barge, he and nine other malefactors who were equally mystified as to how such an evil fate had befallen their magnificent badness.

FOUR

Now:

THE SLITTED GUN port opened. The Q-gun stuck its ugly snout out in the open, and the turret revolved, bringing the weapon to bear on Assistant Deputy Clem Sugarland.

Deputy Sheriff Benedict was making his play.

Clem stood between the cage and a hole in the ground, facing the substation. The hole in the ground led to a subsurface garage holding the station's two patrol vehicles. The entry hatch was open. Clem had planned to remove the vehicles from the garage, replacing them with the barge and its cargo of caged crooks. It would be a tight fit, but it could be done. The station lacked the capacity to hold this many prisoners at one time, but once the hatch was shut, the garage plus the cage would have made a pretty fair mass detention cell. It would have been good enough to hold them until the sheriff arrived with reinforcements to take charge of the prisoners.

Benedict had other ideas. Some of the prisoners started shouting wildly when the turreted Q-gun snapped into the ready firing position. It didn't take a genius to figure out that when one lawman turns against another, the crooks can only benefit from the discord. They were safely out of the line of fire, too.

"Shoot, shoot! Kill him!" they cried.

"Looks like a jailbreak, eh, Mr. Benedict?" Clem said into his comm link.

Benedict did not reply, at least not in words.

He's in for a big surprise when he tries to fire that Q-gun, thought Clem.

Sure enough, clicking and ratcheting noises came from the weapon, signifying that it had been auto-locked and loaded preparatory to firing—all it could do, with the all-important electronic trigger mechanism having been disabled.

But it was Clem who was due for a surprise, for even while he was distracted by the Q-gun, Benedict popped out of the tunnel entrance and shot him with a shock grenade.

The egg-shaped pellet slammed into Clem's armored torso with sledgehammer impact. It made a fist-sized dent in his breastplate and knocked him backward a dozen feet, and that was merely from the concussive effect.

The grenade released its powerful electric charge, enough voltage to kill a dozen unshielded men. Crackling blue fire engulfed Clem from head to toe, vaporizing insulators, melting wires, shorting out his suit defenses. He felt like a lobster being boiled inside its shell.

The discharge grounded, dissipated, ended. Clem fell on his back, twitching and jerking, limbs thrashing.

Benedict came out from behind the cover of the tunnel mouth. He was helmeted and suited up and carried an assault rifle. A wisp of smoke curled from the muzzle of the grenade launcher underslung from the rifle barrel.

Clem's bones ached and his heart pounded as if it would burst. The wind was knocked out of him; he gasped for breath. Trying to move, he succeeded only in lifting his head a few inches from the ground.

His assault rifle lay a few feet away, out of his reach. He still had his sidearm. Summoning up everything he had left, he strained to move his numbed arm to the side, trying to reach the weapon holstered on his hip.

Benedict's assault rifle fired a stuttering burst into Clem's side, smashing the handgun and tearing it loose from the hip holster. Clem writhed under the barrage. Despite the protection from the armor, he felt as though hot rivets were being driven into his flesh. The slugs dented the armor but didn't penetrate it.

The prisoners cheered.

Benedict crossed to Clem. The prisoners were going wild, raising the kind of ruckus that can only be made by condemned men suddenly confronted with an unexpected chance of reprieve.

Benedict stitched a line of shots in the dirt a few inches from the front of the cage.

"Shut up. I'll see to you later," he said, speaking to them through the extro-microphone on his helmet.

They shut up.

Benedict switched channels to the in-helmet comm link, so only Clem could hear what he was saying.

"You didn't think I'd fall for that trick of disarming the firing mechanism of the Q-gun, did you, boy? Hell, I had a spy-eye on you the whole time you were in the vault, hiding the fuses in your kit box. I'll have to trouble you to return them. Can't have the big gun down too long, not with all the desperate characters around these parts."

Clem struggled to raise himself on his elbows. Benedict kicked him in the chest, knocking him flat, then put his foot on the breastplate, pinning him down. He swung the assault rifle muzzle-down, holding it a few inches above Clem's face-plate. The tough polycarbonate visor was bulletproof, but not against assault rifle auto-fire at point-blank range.

"I like it better this way," Benedict said. "If I'd done you with the Q-gun there'd be too many questions. I might even get an official reprimand for carelessness for blasting a brother officer. A black mark on the record could hurt me come promotion time. No, no. Officer Sugarland was killed when a prisoner he was escorting overpowered him and shot him with his own gun. Then I killed the killer. That's how it'll look when I get done fixing things up, anyway."

"You won't . . . get away with it. Too many . . . witnesses."

Benedict laughed. "What witnesses? The prisoners will be long gone, except for the one I pick as the fall guy, and he'll be dead. And the good people of Beamer Junction know to keep their mouths shut. They like living.

"It's kind of tough on me, though. Now I'll have to break in a new assistant. I hope headquarters sends me someone with some smarts next time. You're one of those country boys who's just too damn dumb to be dishonest. Too dumb to live," he said.

Commotion in the cage distracted him from pulling the trigger.

Mars Barton flexed his muscles, breaking his chains as if they were ribbons. Which they were. Grabbing the bar behind him, he gave it a sharp twist, unscrewing it from its threaded socket base. A three-foot-long piece of pipe came loose from the cage's gridded framework, opening a gap in the enclosure.

Tumbling backward out through the hole, still clutching the pipe, Barton rolled onto the hard-baked ground, flattened into a prone position, and pointed one end of the pipe at Benedict. The deputy was still bringing his rifle up and around to counter the threat when Barton cut loose.

What looked like a piece of pipe was actually a disguised beamer tube, a heavy-duty lightning rod with a two-inch bore. A rugged node about a third of the way up from the bottom of the tube was a disguised firing stud. Mars Barton thumbed it on.

A jagged blue bolt arced from the beamer bore to Deputy Benedict. The effect was the same as if he had been struck by lightning, except that this bolt was man-made rather than heaven-sent.

The thunderclap sounded like a bomb going off.

Benedict fell a few feet from Clem. Sand hissed and popped under his super-heated armor. Blue sparks jumped from his suit; smoke wisps curled out from between the flexi-joints of the armored segments.

Clem fought to remain conscious, but lost.

Clem awoke. He lay on his bunk in his private quarters, a closet-sized cubicle tucked under a flange on the main floor of the station. Sitting up too suddenly, he learned that his body was a mass of aches and pains. He lay back down again, all pale and trembling.

Time passed. He tried to get up and succeeded. He was still pale and trembling, but he could function after a fashion as long as he didn't make any sudden moves.

If I was dead, I'd be feeling no pain at all, he told himself. He wasn't dead. Why? Trying to puzzle out the answer made his head hurt even worse than before.

He took stock of himself. Someone had unshelled him from his armor and peeled off his insulated bodysuit. He was in his jumpsuit, which was open above the waist. His ribs were taped up, wound in white gauze that was too neat to have been applied with human hands. It could only have been done by the exacting instruments of the robodoc, which meant that Clem had spent some time in the tank, undergoing its healing ministrations. How much time?

He was able to stay on his feet if he held onto something at the same time or braced himself against the wall. It didn't feel like he had any broken bones. A rubbery looseness in his limbs told him that he was still under the influence of painkillers, which the robodoc must have injected into his bloodstream while he was in the tank. He still hurt like hell, so without the painkillers he probably wouldn't have been able to walk. He couldn't see his chest, where the shock grenade had hit him, because it was taped up, but his right side was one giant purple bruise from hip to kneecap, where Benedict had shot off his sidearm.

And Benedict, what of him? And the prisoners?

Benedict wasn't in the central command post. Clem was alone in the great round room. At a glance, all the equipment seemed to be in working order. If anybody had wanted to sabotage it, they'd have had free run of the place while Clem was blacked out. Console display readouts showed that the station was secure, with all means of entry locked up tight.

Clem limped over to the robodoc, a lifesaving apparatus that looked like an old-fashioned iron lung, with various attachments and display boards. Doctors were hard to come by in the hinterlands, and good doctors were rare as hen's teeth—as rare as hens, for that matter, for in a world of vat-grown protein concentrate and algae-soy ration bars, real poultry was an expensive delicacy reserved for the privileged few.

The robodoc was an emergency hospital in a machine. The patient would stretch out lengthwise in the cylinder, and after that the machine did all the rest. Even a critically injured individual had a good chance of surviving if he or she managed to get in the cylinder, a feature much appreciated by fighting units supplied with the machine. Once inside, the patient would be properly positioned by mechanical lifters and rollers. The upper half of the cylinder would close, sealing shut, enclosing the subject in a sterile, germ-free environment. Air was pumped in, along with anesthetic sprays if needed. A web of sensors monitored vital signs, continually relaying to the robodoc's computerized guidance unit, which would diagnose the problem and initiate treatment. An array of sophisticated servomechanisms would cut off garments to get to the injured areas, then slice, stitch, disinfect, repair, inject, bandage, and do whatever else was needed to mend the patient. Statistics proved that robodocs killed a lot less patients than did real flesh-and-blood physicians.

A scroll of graph paper lay in rolls at the foot of the machine, which had output it in hard copy. Clem checked it out. It charted his condition with lots of numbers and arrows and squiggly lines. He had trouble making heads or tails out of it, but as far as he could tell, it looked like he was going to live.

He took a sidearm and gunbelt from the armory. He was too sore to wear them on his hip, so he looped the gunbelt over a shoulder, with the holstered weapon hanging under his arm, butt-out. Clem felt better with a gun near at hand.

He could investigate the situation a lot better from a seat at the control console than by dragging himself from room to room. He started to take his usual seat, thought better of it, and lowered himself into the commander's chair.

Every square inch of the station and its environs was covered by spy-eye cameras. Viewscreens displayed what the cameras saw. Switching from camera to camera, Clem could search the station room by room without ever leaving his chair.

What he saw in the underground garage made him adjust the settings so that all the viewscreens displayed different camera angles of the same scene.

The patrol vehicles had been taken from the garage to make room for the cageful of crooks. It was still on the barge, which now rested on the floor. The hole in the cage had been repaired, patched with some metalloy pry bars that had been hastily but effectively welded into place by an industrial burner. It was an added precaution, perhaps unnecessary, for the chains shackling the prisoners still held them rooted in place.

The unhappy captives were quieter now, for the most part, apathy having succeeded over frustrated rage in their emotions, although a few were still ranting and raving. They still numbered ten in all, but there had been a slight change in personnel.

Mars Barton was gone, nowhere to be seen; his place in the cage was now filled by Deputy Sheriff Benedict, alive and in chains.

Former Deputy Sheriff Benedict. Clem was so flabbergasted by the turn of events that it wasn't until much later that he finally noticed the badge that had been pinned to his jumpsuit: the deputy's badge that had belonged to Benedict.

"If that don't beat all!" Clem said.

FIVE

"AFTER THAT I called you, you came, and that's all there is to tell," Clem said.

"It's the damnedest story I've ever heard," Sheriff Thornton said.

"That's how it happened, just like I told it."

"Oh, don't get me wrong, Sugarland, I believe you. It's just that the whole business has got me baffled."

Clem couldn't hide his disappointment. "I was hoping that you'd have the answers, Sheriff. That this was some kind of top-secret operation that the department was running."

"I wish it was! I'd be proud to be part of rounding up some of the most dangerous crooks in seven counties. But I'm as much in the dark about it as you are," Thornton said.

Clem turned to the other two visitors who had accompanied the sheriff into the privacy of the Beamer Junction station to be briefed on the unprecedented incident that had happened earlier this day.

"Maybe you gentlemen have some idea of what it's all about?" he said.

"Sorry, but it's as much of a mystery to us as it is to you," Inspector Otto Scoob said.

His companion, Dan Guthrie, didn't say anything, but nodded in agreement.

The four of them were seated around the mess table in an alcove on the main floor of the substation, opposite the

control console. Outside, it was night, sometime between
sunset and midnight. The badmen were still there, caged
and confined in the underground motor pool, but soon to
be shipped to the jail at headquarters in Middletown, the
county seat.

Responding to Clem's radioed SOS, Sheriff Thornton
had led a flying squad out to Beamer Junction to secure the
situation. The squad was aboveground, manning a defensive
perimeter they had thrown up around the station to guard it
against any full-scale assault the friends (if any) or accom-
plices (more likely) of the caged crooks might unleash, to
free them or, barring that, kill them to silence them.

Three men and the Judge had listened to Clem tell his
story. Orlando Thornton was the duly elected sheriff of the
county and Clem's boss. Square-faced, with a banana nose
and a wide, loose mouth, he was nominally in charge of the
situation.

With him were two important persons from Commissioner Piper's office in Santone. Santone wasn't even in
this county, but it was the biggest city in twenty-seven
counties and its shadow loomed large throughout South
Texas. Inspector Otto Scoob was the chief investigator for
the Santone police's PIU, the Political Intelligence Unit.
Dan Guthrie was a special investigator working directly for
Commissioner Piper, the de facto Baron of Santone. Scoob
did most of the talking for the two of them, but he deferred
to Guthrie, who far and away had the most clout of anyone
on the scene.

The Judge sat in the middle of the table, evaluating
the truthfulness of Clem's deposition, which he gave as
sworn testimony. The Judge was a machine about the size
and shape of a laptop computer, a portable lie detector
containing a built-in voice stress analyzer, galvanic skin
response meter, heartbeat and respiration rate monitor, and
a number of functions whose purpose was to determine
if the subject was telling the truth or a lie. No impartial
arbiter of truth, it measured the teller, seeking the giveaway
signs of involuntary stress that accompany the telling of
what the subject knows to be a deliberate falsehood. Like

the polygraphs of old, it was not infallible. If a lunatic professed that the moon was made of green cheese and sincerely believed it, the Judge's verdict would be that the subject was telling the truth. Likewise, while it took certain measures to detect the use of hypnotic suggestion and other mindbenders, sophisticated brainwashing techniques were beyond its ability to detect.

It was no mark against Clem's credibility that the Judge was in operation while he spoke. That was standard operating procedure whenever sworn testimony was being given. In Texas, an individual had the right to decline being evaluated by the Judge. The Judge's verdict was inadmissable in a court of law, but refusal to be examined was a fact that could be introduced as evidence, and was often interpreted by jurors as a tacit admission of guilt.

Clem readily accepted the option of "telling it to the Judge." He had nothing to hide—and such was the verdict that the Judge passed on his testimony.

"I'd like to ask Officer Sugarland one or two more questions if you don't mind, Sheriff," Scoob said.

"Sure, go ahead. Anything that'll help get to the bottom of this is fine with me."

"Thanks," Scoob said. "I know you've had a long day, Clem—you don't mind if I call you 'Clem,' do you? I know you must be tired and you'd like to get some rest, Clem, so I'll try to keep this as short as possible."

"Shucks, I don't mind, Inspector. This must be pretty important for the Commissioner of Santone to take an interest in it."

"It is important, Clem. I can't tell you much more than that, because it's classified, but I can say that Mr. Piper appreciates your cooperation in this matter. Now, then, there's a few points I'd like to clarify. One is this cruiser that some of the prisoners spoke of. Did you see it?"

"No, sir. Not with my own eyes."

"What about the detectors? Did they track it?"

"No. Not a blip."

"Were there any unusual readings, little things, maybe, like a cloud or flock of birds? Something you might have thought was a glitch, or a misreading caused by interference, or a mag storm, or something like that?"

"No. The first thing we picked up was the barge when it entered the range of the detector."

"What about evidence of energy discharges? Specifically, use of an energy weapon of class 2 or higher?"

"The only E-wep besides Mr. Benedict's was the beamer tube launcher that knocked him out, and that was a class 1. Close to the max for that class, Inspector, but still just a plain old class 1."

Scoob sat back, rubbing his chin, squeezing his cheeks so his lips stuck out like a Kewpie doll's. After a pause, he leaned forward again.

"Was there any advance notice, any kind of warning at all that something like this was going to happen?" he said.

"No, sir, it came out of the blue."

"Now, this could be important, so I'd like you to think it over a moment before giving your answer. Has anything happened in the Junction or hereabouts in the last few weeks that was somehow unusual, out of the ordinary? It could be something that seems completely unrelated to this matter, some sort of unusual phenomenon that deviated from the everyday routine in this jurisdiction?"

"Things happen in the Junction but they're not what you'd call unusual, Inspector. We get a few killings a week and a lot of assault and theft cases, but it's all mostly small-time stuff."

"Umph."

"There was something about a week ago, though," Clem said after a pause. "I'm not sure it's what you're looking for, but it was something different that kind of stuck in my mind at the time."

"What was it, Clem?"

"Well, a couple of scrap metal scavengers were out prospecting around Shatterbridge—that's about twenty-five miles southeast of here—"

"I know where it is," Sheriff Thornton said.

"Anyway, the two of them—Caveman Wellington and Roz Mendoza, their names are—came into town scared and in a hurry. They'd been camped out there for a few days, until they saw something that scared them into clearing out of their diggings fast."

"What was that?" Scoob said.

"Claimed they'd seen an APU." "Ah-poo," is how Clem pronounced it.

"An autonomic patrol unit?" Guthrie said, speaking for the first time in a long while.

"You mean one of those old-time robot prowl cars, the kind with a human brain in them?" Thornton said.

"Not so old, Sheriff. Last I heard, there were still a few of them around, as recently as five years ago," Guthrie said.

"That's when they were all retired," Scoob said.

"Every now and then you hear stories about a few of them that never came in, that are still roaming the boonies," Guthrie said.

"That's what Wellington and Mendoza said. They claimed they saw one crossing the old dry riverbed at dusk and hightailed it out of there fast. I don't know what they saw, but that's what they thought they saw and the Judge said they weren't lying. They're rumdums and troublemakers and they'd take any drug they could get their hands on, like most scavengers when they're in town, but they sure saw something. Mr. Benedict thought that they hallucinated the whole thing, but he sent me out there for a look-see anyway, just in case."

"Did you find anything, Clem?"

"Tracks, Inspector, I found tracks. Tracks of a six-wheeled vehicle that came out of the flats northwest of town on the other side of the divide, cut south to the dry river, and followed the west bank until it found a shallow enough cut to get down to the riverbed a few miles south of Shatterbridge. That's where the scavengers saw it. It followed the bed until it found a cut that let it climb to the east bank, then curved southeast for about six, seven miles before hitting Rocky Plain. The trail ended at the rocks, at least I couldn't follow it anymore. There was no vehicle in range of the detectors, and the trail was too cold for the infrared sensors to pick up anything, so I headed back. Fuel's precious and I figured I had already wasted enough on what could turn out to be a wild goose chase."

"But was it an APU?"

"Maybe yes, maybe no. The tires that made the tracks could've been from a prowler, but they could just as well have come from an ordinary all-terrain vehicle."

"Six wheels, eh? Kind of small for a patrol unit. Most of them were big monsters with twelve, sometimes sixteen wheels. A lot of them had treads," the sheriff said.

"There were some six-wheelers," Guthrie said. "Scouts, mostly. And it's the smaller ones that are supposed to still be on the loose. The big ones were retired first because they used so much fuel and they were easiest to find."

He sat backward, with his arms folded across the top of the back of the chair. Six feet, two inches tall, rangy, and broad-shouldered, he kept himself in fine athletic trim despite being on the far side of fifty. His thick, dark rooster-comb pompadour was touched with gray only at the temples. His eyes turned up at the corners and his mouth turned down, giving him a sardonic expression even when his features were at rest. He wore plain clothes, rugged but expensive: a quilted gray jacket with bulky wristband cuffs, a black pullover sweater, and baggy brown trousers tucked into ankle-high antishock boots. A well-worn gunbelt was buckled across his waist, its fast-draw swing-out holster sheathing a snub-nosed machine pistol. The weapon was top-of-the-line hardware, with gleaming gray-black metalloy surfaces and a retro wooden-handled grip. It was a lot of gun to handle even with the standard-issue long barrel, but it took a strong and sure marksman to wield the snub model. The short-barreled machine pistol was a gunfighter's weapon, designed for fast-draw, close-quarters combat.

Dan Guthrie. Clem had never heard of him, but Santone was a long way off and Commissioner Piper's agents kept a low profile. The sheriff and Inspector Scoob sure treated Guthrie like he was a somebody, though.

"I made some 3-D holographic casts of the tire tracks. They're on file, if you'd like to see them," Clem said.

"I'd like. Take care of it, Otto. Make some copies," Guthrie said.

"Right, Dan," Scoob said.

"Reckon there's some connection between the APU and the stranger, Mr. Guthrie?"

"I don't know, but I can't afford to overlook any possible tie-in, no matter how flukey it might seem. Even if it's a coincidence, a rogue APU is nothing to sneeze about. Those prowlers carry a lot of firepower and even a small one can do plenty of damage. The scavengers who made the sighting, are they still in town?"

"Wellington and Mendoza? No, sir. You know how prospectors are, they only come into town for supplies or to go on a tear. As soon as they saw there wasn't any reward money coming their way, they got out of town fast. They won't be working the diggings out by Shatterbridge too soon, is my guess. The prowler scared them but good. I've got their statements on file, though."

"I'd like copies of them, too. That was some smart police work on your part, Sugarland."

"Just routine, Mr. Guthrie, but thanks. You know plenty about police work yourself. You a lawman?"

"I used to be. Now I'm working in a more administrative capacity," Guthrie said. "That deputy's badge you're wearing is liable to become permanent, if Thornton here's got as much sense as I think he has."

"My sentiments exactly," Thornton said. "With Benedict out of the picture, Sugarland's acting deputy sheriff anyway, so I don't see why the position shouldn't be made permanent."

"Well, thanks, Sheriff, I really appreciate it. It's a real honor for me. I wasn't trying to promote myself by wearing the deputy's badge. I wouldn't even have thought of putting it on myself—"

"Tut tut, think nothing of it, *Deputy* Sugarland."

"Thanks again, Sheriff." Clem's face burned and he wondered if he was blushing.

"Congratulations, Clem. You deserve it."

"Thanks, Inspector."

"I wish we had a hundred more like you on the force in Santone. If you ever get tired of working for the sheriff, there's a job waiting for you over in my bailiwick."

"That's real big of you, Inspector, but I'm happy right here working for the sheriff's department, especially as a deputy."

Clem fingered the badge pinned on his chest. "Who'd have thunk that Mars Barton would've put a deputy's star on me? 'Course, it couldn't have really been the Red Planet Man himself. It must have been an imposter pretending to be him. From what I hear, the real Barton ain't exactly what you'd call a Good Samaritan. Wonder what happened to him, anyhow?"

"Probably in an unmarked grave somewhere," Scoob said.

"One more thing, Deputy. Any ideas on where the APU might have been heading?"

"Well, Mr. Guthrie, once it got on the rocks, it could have gone a lot of ways, since the plain stretches out in all directions for many a mile. But if it kept on course to the southeast, eventually it'd turn up somewhere around Mountain, is my guess."

Guthrie and Scoob exchanged glances, but whatever the significance of the information, Thornton was out of the loop, the data holding no particular meaning for him.

"Did I say something wrong?" Clem asked, looking from Guthrie to Scoob.

"No, just interesting," Guthrie said. "Fact is, Mountain's what you might call a business competitor of Santone's. If a rogue prowler is headed their way, they're welcome to it. It's their headache."

"We'll notify them to be on the lookout for it, of course," Scoob added.

"Naturally," Guthrie said, showing his teeth in what was supposed to be a smile.

A light flashed in the ruby ring Guthrie wore on the ring finger of his left hand. "Excuse me, I'm wanted on my personal communicator," he said.

He rose from his chair, walked a half-dozen paces, and halted with his back turned to the others. From an inside jacket pocket he took out his personal comm link, a thin, curved white-plastic headset with an earpiece at one end and a mini-mike at the other. He fit the earphone into his left ear, so that the miniaturized microphone rested a few inches from his lips.

The others respected his privacy by pointedly looking elsewhere as the message came in. Clem glanced at the gauges and dials of the control console's instrument panel. They remained unchanged, indicating that the incoming message was being transmitted on an ultra-secure tight-beam carrier wave, undetectable by standard monitoring hardware.

Guthrie's shoulders stiffened as he got the news, whatever it was. His part of the conversation consisted of a few curt, monosyllabic replies.

"I'll get back to you," he said at last, ending the dialogue. He folded the headset and put it back in his pocket.

"Problems, Dan?"

"Nothing but problems in this life, Otto," Guthrie said.

Moving his chair so that it was opposite Clem's, on the other side of the table, Guthrie sat down, resting his folded hands on the table. The fingers of his right hand toyed idly with the heavy, segmented wristband cuff of his left sleeve.

He smiled at Clem. Clem smiled back. Guthrie pressed a stud on his wristband.

A cough of compressed air sounded as the wristband dart launcher shot a hair-fine sliver into Clem's eye. Piercing the eyeball, it penetrated the socket, burying itself deep in his brain. A pinpoint explosive tip detonated, causing instant death while a smile was still frozen on Clem's face.

He flopped backward, taking the chair with him. His knees slammed the underside of the table. Clem and the chair crashed to the floor.

"Damn!" Thornton shouted, shocked and frightened.

Scoob was startled, too, but Thornton's outburst covered his reaction, giving him time to get his feelings under control.

Thornton jumped up, overturning his chair as he went around the table to drop to one knee beside Clem. Clem lay on his back, still smiling. His eyeball was punctured, and a thin worm of black blood was inching out of the corner of the socket, but apart from that there was very little gore, the explosive's damage having been confined to the core of the brain.

"Dead! Why'd you kill him?!" Thornton said.

"He was a loose end. It's tied up now," Guthrie said.

"I thought you said it wouldn't do any harm to leave him alive, as long as he was stuck in this jerkwater town in the middle of nowhere," Scoob said.

"Going soft, Otto?"

Guthrie's voice was low, mocking. Whatever Scoob heard in it, he didn't like it.

"Soft? Hell, no, Dan, you know me! I don't care how many have to die, I was just surprised, that's all, since you said that there was no need to kill him."

"That was before, Otto. Things changed."

"That message you got—"

"Shhhh," Guthrie said, putting a finger across his lips. "Don't think out loud, Otto. The sheriff might hear something he shouldn't and then he'd have to be gotten rid of, too."

"I—You wouldn't! I didn't hear anything, Mr. Guthrie, I swear it!"

"Relax, Thornton. You're safe enough for now. You're going to get this mess squared away and put the right spin on it."

"Sure, Mr. Guthrie, sure, anything you say! Only—what is the right spin? I'm kind of confused . . ."

"You can say that again. But don't worry, I'll tell you how to handle it. Sugarland died from wounds received in the line of duty—that's how the reports will read. It's true enough, at that."

"We three are the only ones who saw him alive since he radioed for help. The squad topside never got a look at him, so we're covered there," Scoob offered helpfully.

"Now you're thinking, Otto," Guthrie said. "That's the kind of straight-ahead, problem-solving kind of thinking we need at a time like this, eh, Sheriff?"

"Yeah. What about the prisoners, you still taking them back to Santone with you?"

"Afraid there's been a change of plans there, too, Sheriff. Something came up that doesn't leave me with a lot of time to crap around with them. I've got bigger fish to fry."

"The county jail in Middletown isn't big enough to hold those hombres, Mr. Guthrie. We don't have the manpower or the firepower."

"Who said anything about holding them?"

"You don't mean—"

"Texas will have to get along with ten less badmen. Too bad about the outdated hardware the station's equipped with. It failed to detect a booby trap hidden in the barge. Must have been planted there by radicals, anarchists, maybe, or some of those Zeeg nuts. The barge is a Trojan horse, see, bait in a trap set by some cop haters. Lucky the bomb went off in the underground motor pool, otherwise a lot more people would have gotten killed. As it was, the only casualties were the crooks and brave Deputy Sugarland. There wasn't enough left of the corpses to autopsy. Think you can remember all that, Sheriff?"

"Sure, Mr. Guthrie, sure, only where can I get a bomb? The department's arsenal has grenades and mortar rounds, but nothing much bigger than that."

"We'll take care of that. We'll fly it in from Santone. It should be here within the hour. A pound of deccanite should do it, eh, Otto?"

"And then some."

"A pound of deccanite will turn this station to atoms!"

"So what? The county will have to build a new one, which means there'll be plenty of opportunities for some good old-fashioned graft and kickbacks for you, Sheriff."

"You've got something there, Mr. Guthrie. But, uh, there's some pretty big rewards on some of the prisoners . . ."

"They're wanted dead or alive. Technically they'll be in your custody when they get blown up, so you're still entitled to the bounties. Otto and I will testify to back up your claim, so you won't have any trouble collecting the reward."

"Well, thanks. That's mighty generous of you."

"Consider it a bonus for a job well done."

"I'd hate to have to tell it to the Judge, though."

"Nobody's going to ask any questions. The state will be glad to be saved the expense of ten trials, and a lot of big people will be damned glad that none of the guilty lived long enough to incriminate them."

"It sounds simple enough the way you tell it, Mr. Guthrie."

"It is simple, Sheriff, as long as you follow the plan and don't try to get cute."

"Not me. I'm happy to just do as I'm told."

"Good. Stay happy and you'll be healthy, wealthy, and alive," Guthrie said.

His tone indicated that the briefing was over. He got up from his chair.

"Let's go, Otto, we've got things to do. We can rest easy knowing that this situation is in Sheriff Thornton's capable hands," he said.

"Too bad about Sugarland. I kind of liked the boy."

"Hell, Otto, so did I, but that's the way the deal went down. Anyway, he didn't have much of a future with the department. Too honest."

"Well, at least it was fast."

"Sure, he never knew what hit him. That's the way to go if you've got to go, and he had to go. And he died a deputy, so his kin will get paid death benefits at that rating. You'll make sure of that, Sheriff."

"You bet, Mr. Guthrie. I'll even put him in for a medal for valor—posthumous, of course."

"See that you do."

• • •

The vertical and standard takeoff and landing (V/STOL) Raptor aircraft that had flown Guthrie and Scoob out from Santone stood parked in the lee of the station's aboveground half-dome, inside the defensive perimeter that had been established by the sheriff's men. It was guarded by Val Ketchum and Cholly Maldonado, two of Scoob's men. They were Silversuits, members of the elite SWAT team of the Santone Police Department—the much feared and hated "Silverfish" of underworld parlance. Neutral-toned lightweight jumpsuits covered the glittering argent metal-mesh bodysuits from which the unit had taken its name. Guthrie and Scoob wore silver suits under their clothes, too. So did the pilot, who was smoking and stretching his legs near the Raptor.

Guthrie's nodded command sent the pilot scrambling into the cockpit to start warming up the plane for takeoff. Breedlove and Maldonado stood by for their orders, while Guthrie took Scoob under the curved underside of the hull to give him his special instructions.

Guthrie switched on a hand-held detector. The needles on the dials remained inert; no spy rays or audio intercepts were in use against him. He hadn't expected that they would be, but he was a cautious man. It helped him to stay alive.

Contact! The Raptor's twin engines turned over, roaring into life, fueled by an enriched liquid propellant that was the nearest commercial equivalent to rocket fuel.

Guthrie and Scoob had to put their heads together and shout to be heard over the noise, and no one standing more than an arm's length away could have heard them.

"Beamer Junction is history," Guthrie said.

"The whole town?"

"Sure! It's a small town. Cities will burn before we're through, so get used to it."

"I don't care. You sending in the Punishment Platoon?"

"No need. A squad of Nightmen will do for Thornton and his people. The Hostiles can take care of the townfolk. Pass the word to Bronco; he'll know what to do. I want his shock troops massed outside town ready for action no later than 0300 hours and out of here by 0400."

"The Hostiles won't like that, Dan. It doesn't leave them much time for fun and games."

"Tough. This is business, not pleasure. You stay here and make sure that everything gets taken care of."

"Right."

"Ketchum's coming with me. Maldonado will stay here and cover you until the Nightmen come. You'll all be back in Santone before dawn."

"You coming back here?"

"No. I'm going down to Salt Lick and I don't know when I'll be back."

"Salt Lick? Doesn't ring a bell, Dan."

"It's a little shithole in the Badlands near Mountain."

"Uh-oh. Trouble?"

"Nothing but trouble in this world, Otto. It looks like our advance men managed to fuck things up pretty good down there."

"Nothing serious, I hope!"

"Nothing that this can't fix," Guthrie said, patting his sidearm.

SIX

THE YAHOOS WERE wilding in Molehill this night. It was bad for business for the after-dark vice trade, but there was little that the organized crime bosses could do about it except write off their losses as part of the price of maintaining the delicate truce that existed between them and the local gangs.

Molehill was a vast sprawling slum district that existed in the shadow of Mountain, a walled city on the eastern border of the Badlands in Southwest Texas, near the border. Texas was mostly flat plains, but there were mountains in this part of the state, or at least big hills that topped off in the 1,500- to 2,250-foot range. They could be seen on the horizon from the new city, which had taken its name from them. Mountain was a boom town which had grown strong and rich due to its proximity to the Border and the Badlands. It was a key point on the overland trade routes from the mining towns of the mineral-rich Badlands, and on the equally lucrative smuggling trails into and out of Mexico.

Mountain was a fortress city, walled, gated, and well policed. Admittance was restricted to registered citizens, although short-term visitor's passes were issued to select, officially sponsored nonresidents, allowing them entry to most sectors of the city. Those persons necessary to the maintenance and continuing prosperity of Mountain were permitted to dwell with their families in residential districts inside the city walls.

Such elaborate security precautions were the rule rather than the exception in the world of A.D. 2035—doubly so in the Southwest Border Badlands, one of the most dangerous zones on the North American continent. Three foreign armies and countless guerrilla and counterrevolutionary forces plagued the sierra of Upper Mexico and the Yucatan peninsula, frequently raiding across the border. The mountains and the Vulcan Belt also harbored bandits, marauders, nomadic biker horders, cultists, fugitives, hermits, madmen, and other assorted antisocial types.

The eternal conflict between the haves and the have-nots had escalated into a shooting war. In the Mountain area, the haves lived in the walled city, and the have-nots lived in Molehill.

Molehill's masses supplied Mountain with a pool of unskilled labor that could be tapped as needed. Molehill was also a source of illicit thrills for high and low society alike. Sex, drugs, gambling, weapons, the extremes of pain and pleasure, all were available for the right price.

Glitter Gulch was the heart of the vice district, a gaudy neon-lit strip jammed with casinos, bars, drug dens, brothels, black medicine clinics, laser-print tattoo parlors, sexarenas, bootleg software vendors, pornatoriums, pawnshops, torture palaces, pedo-parks, illegal arms dealers, stolen goods bazaars, flophouses, hot sheet hotels, and other, less mainstream attractions.

The venues of Glitter Gulch were licensed to operate by the regional branch of the Syndicate, an interlocking combination of the Texas mob, the Mexicrime cartel, the Vietnamerican BTKs, the Gulf Coast Triad, and a loose amalgam of powerful independent local outfits. Too big to be bothered with micro-managing so many small businesses, the Syndicate raked off a hefty percentage of the take in exchange for buying off the police. But there was another power in Molehill that the Syndicate preferred not to confront, and that was the youth gangs.

There were over ten thousand hardcore gang members in the slum district, all of them armed with automatic weapons at the very least, while many in the leadership cadres and death squads had access to energy weapons and high explosives. Molehill was a crazy quilt of small pieces of turf, each controlled by its own neighborhood gang. The gangs' main interests were fighting and hell-raising; lacking the discipline to run anything but small-time rackets, they were no competition for the big-time mobsters. But they made fearsome foes when crossed. The young warriors, many of them barely into their teens, had nothing to lose but their miserable lives, which they valued barely a shade more than the lives of others, which they valued not at all. Gangbangers and racketeers coexisted in an uneasy truce in their parallel worlds, ignoring each other as much as possible. On the rare occasions that they clashed, the results were brutal, the slaughter immense.

Glitter Gulch was an independent entity, a sovereign state located in the heart of Maddog territory. Maddog was one of the most powerful gangs in Molehill. Their prestige was such that the Syndicate had entered into an informal working arrangement with them. It was cheaper to buy them off than wipe them out. Besides, if the Maddogs were liquidated, which wouldn't be easy, a rival gang would inevitably arise to take their place. So the Syndicate stroked them with regular payments of drugs and small arms in return for the gang's respecting the inviolability of the Gulch. An added benefit was that the Maddogs allowed Gulch clientele safe passage more or less through their turf. It was a good deal for both sides, but mistakes happened . . .

Trouble was inevitable when the Yahoos got hold of a half-brick of Aggro. The Yahoos were a kind of junior auxiliary to the Maddog Posse, cubs in training for the senior wolf pack. The Aggro came to them by accident, when a magnetic storm interrupted the directional signals from an orbiting navigation beacon satellite. A long-haul suspensor barge trucker got separated from the rest of his convoy en route to Mountain to deliver construction equipment. The lost big-rig barge strayed outside the transportation corridor and crash landed in an old bomb crater left over from the last war. The crater was in Maddog territory, in one of the dead zones of ruined city blocks. *Primo* scavengers, the Yahoos had been all over the wrecked barge almost as soon as it hit the ground. The trucker was killed in the crash, spoiling some of the Yahoos' fun. Disappointment turned to glee when they discovered the stash of Aggro hidden in the operator's cab.

Aggro was a drug much used and abused by long-haul drivers and others who pulled marathon work shifts with minimal sleep periods. The dead trucker was a user, which may have explained why he had been killed in a fatal accident. He was not only a user but a small-time pusher, since the half-brick of Aggro he carried was enough for him and the rest of the convoy to drive nonstop to Tierra del Fuego.

Known as "the poor man's Ferol," Aggro was a compound of mega-methamphetamine, PCP, STP, and whatever synthetic steroids the makers happened to have on hand when they were brewing up the latest batch. Ferol was derived from actual human glandular extracts and required a fairly sophisticated biochemical process to produce, while Aggro could be whipped up by bathtub chemists without too much fuss. A body drug that suppressed fatigue, pain, and fear, Aggro was much in demand by the rank-and-file soldiers of crimedom. Ferol was their drug of choice, but Aggro was much cheaper and easier to get.

The Yahoo scavengers knew what they were supposed to do: turn their find over to a Maddog youth liasion, who would give them a small cut while passing the bulk of the booty on to his superiors. Harsh penalties awaited those who tried to hold out from the higher-ups. But the Yahoos decided to do a taste of the drug first, and once the Aggro hit their bloodstreams, caution and all other inhibitions went flying out the window.

By nightfall, a couple hundred Yahoos were running wild in an Aggro-fueled orgy of rape, violence, and murder.

"How much farther do we have to go?" Carstairs said.

"Not far," Rima said.

"You said that before."

"We're almost there. And once we get there, you can go as far as you like."

"Now you're talking."

"As long as you pay for it," she added.

"Everything in the Gulch has its price, huh?"

"That's right. That's why you came here. I hope you're not one of those tightwads. I like generous gentlemen."

"I don't mind spending some hard dollars, as long as it's worth it."

"Hard dollars" meant real currency, as opposed to the electronic transfer of funds by Universal credit cards, which was the way most legitimate business dealings were transacted. Uni-cards were few and far between among the denizens of Molehill, or anywhere outside the walled cities.

"You knew I was worth it the minute you saw me," Rima said.

"Maybe so, maybe so."

Carstairs turned, reached for her, pressed against her. The full rounded softness of her lush young body was covered by skintight, paper-thin garments. His hands rubbed her back, moving downward, stroking her sides, hips, thighs.

She let him feel her just long enough to get him steamed up before she slipped out of his embrace.

"Are you making love to me or frisking me?" she said.

"Maybe both."

"Don't you trust me?"

He laughed. She wasn't offended. Trust was even rarer than credit cards in Molehill.

They were in a dim passageway. A retaining wall, fifteen feet high, rose on the left. It was so old that it was made of concrete, its surfaces pitted and worn away. On the right, well-rusted rolls of scalpel-bladed concertina wire were strung from slanting fence posts. On the other side of the wire, an earthen gully sloped down to an old U-shaped culvert whose bottom was filled with a shallow, stagnant trickle of liquid toxic waste. Foul-smelling fumes rose from it; no plants, not even the hardiest weeds, grew in the gully.

The passageway was wide enough for two to walk abreast, and had many twists and turns. The far end, by which the couple had entered some twenty-five yards back, opened on a lonely and deserted side street that ran parallel to the back of the buildings on the north side of Glitter Gulch.

Rima took Carstairs's hand; his palm was sweaty. She started forward. "Come on, let's go," she said.

Fumes from the toxic stream burned his nostrils and brought tears to his eyes.

"Whew! That's raw," he said.

"That's what keeps the people away. It gets better."

"Christ, I hope so. Wait a second, will you."

"It's your time and your money, mister."

Carstairs reached into an inside breast pocket of his jacket. Rima tensed, then eased up when she saw him take out a handkerchief. He covered his nose and mouth with it, knotting the ends behind the back of his head.

"Kinky," she said. "Feel better now?"

"It helps. I don't see how you can stand the stink."

"I'm used to it. You get used to it, living around here."

Rima fidgeted, shifting her weight from one spike-heeled ankle boot to the other. She couldn't help glancing over her shoulder, back the way they had come.

"Nervous?" Carstairs said.

"You bet your ass I'm nervous. If the Streetwalkers Guild catches me poaching on their turf, they'll fix it so no man will ever want to be with me again."

A shudder sent her breasts jiggling against the see-through mesh of her cat suit.

"How come you're not a member?" Carstairs asked, his voice muffled by the kerchief mask.

He rubbed her breasts with one hand and kneaded her buttocks with the other.

"Seems to me you could pass the Guild physical with no trouble," he said.

"I'm the romantic type. I don't want to trick for a living. I like to have some choice, too. Those gals have to do it with anybody who's got the money. With me, the guy's got to turn me on, too. Like you."

"I turn you on?"

"Sure, you're getting me all wet."

"You turn me on, too."

Carstairs took her hand and pressed it against his crotch, rubbing it.

"Ummm, that's a big one . . ."

"I'll bet you say that to all the guys."

"Only if they have big ones like you. Come on, I want to get down on that longhorn of yours."

"What's wrong with doing it right here?"

"It's nicer at this place I know. Smells better, too, away from this toxic shit. Come on, we're almost there."

"We better be, I'm getting so damned horny I can't wait much longer."

"Just a little ways more, and then it's party time," she said.

Rima was a teenage hustler, short, stocky, muscled like a gymnast, big-breasted and broad-bottomed. Her face was almost as wide as it was long, strong-featured, attractive but not pretty. Hard. Her dark eyes were long and slightly slanted, her thick-lipped mouth was painted cherry-red. Her long, thick mane of hair was fashionably zebra-striped in black and gold; she wore it in Minoan-revival style, pulled up and through a six-inch glitterized plastic coronet, then down in a ponytail, reaching to the small of her back. A metalloy circlet as wide as a compact disc secured the end of the ponytail, weighing it down so she always knew where it was. Her cat suit had a velcro-flapped crotchpiece that could be opened from her navel to the top of her buttocks, accessing everything in between. Rima was Molehill.

Carstairs was Mountain, though he worked to disguise the fact. He was about ten years Rima's senior, a still-young man with old eyes. He wore a rugged quilted long coat, a turtleneck sweater under baggy bib overalls, and heavy work boots. He was an up-and-coming functionary in the Ministry of Mineral Trading, assistant to a department head. He had a taste for thrills that couldn't be found in the walled city, and was tough enough and smart enough—and lucky enough—to have made a number of forays into Molehill's pleasure precinct and lived to return again.

Being with Rima was risky, since she was a non-Guild freelance whore. But Carstairs had it on good authority that all the "safe" brothels in Glitter Gulch kept videotaped records of their unsuspecting clients in action, for possible future blackmail attempts. A Ministry official had to have a clean slate, at least he did if he was middle-management level or below. Above that, he could do as he pleased. Carstairs meant to reach that exalted status, and his ascent wasn't to be jeopardized by letting the Gulch vice lords get their hooks into him. Even the registered Guild street-walkers were no good, since the hot sheet hotels where they turned their tricks were undoubtedly also filled with hidden spy-eye cameras.

The path took a slight jog and terminated in a blank wall a stone's throw away. Carstairs's face got ugly; his hand plunged inside the bib apron of his overalls, closing on a flat burner clipped to the waistband.

But it wasn't a dead-end trap, as he had suspected. The barrier only looked solid at first glance. A cleft in the wall opened at waist height and continued upward to the top.

Carstairs wiped the scowl from his face but kept his hand on the burner. Rima tried to make like she didn't know what he was doing.

"It's just on the other side," she said.

"You go first."

"Sure, but you'll come first."

Plastering a broad smile on her face, she started up the mound of rubble at the foot of the cleft.

"Never mind, I'll go first," he said.

"You're the boss."

Cautiously he peeked through the hole in the wall. On the other side was an open space about a half-mile long and a quarter-mile wide, once the site of an eight-lane highway overpass. Now it was a field of stones, rubble, and ashes. The great span had collapsed, leaving behind rubble mounds as big as houses and splintered slabs as big as ships. An eerie moonscape, streaked with a pastel rainbow of colored lights reflected from Glitter Gulch to the south.

Carstairs liked it. He couldn't find this sort of scene in shiny new Mountain.

Rima took his hand and led him down a low rock-strewn ridge to the flat, on which the ground was hard-packed clay where it wasn't covered with dirt piles and ash heaps. They halted where fallen columns formed a kind of three-sided courtyard, open on the fourth side. The tumbled pillars were broken into segments that were about five feet tall.

They were far enough away from the toxic stream that Carstairs's eyes didn't sting anymore. He pulled down his kerchief mask. The air wasn't fragrant, but at least it didn't hurt to breathe it.

The moon was a pale yellow smudge riding high in the hazy night sky. Streamers of mist crossed it.

"Nice, huh?" Rima said.

"Nice."

He reached for her, closing his arms around her. She leaned into him. She closed her hands behind the back of his neck and hung onto him. He grabbed her buttocks, one in each hand, and squeezed them. His fingers felt for the velcro fastenings of her crotchpiece.

She eased out of the embrace, took a step back, and held out her hand palm-up.

"Business before pleasure," she said.

Shrugging, he reached for the buttoned-down flap of the pocket holding his money folder. With his hand in his pocket he froze at the sound of movement in the darkness.

"What's that?" he said.

"Huh? What?"

"That noise."

"I didn't hear anything."

"I did."

"You're hearing things—"

"Shut up," he said.

He stood there, listening, alert.

"I don't hear anything," Rima said.

"Well, I did."

"It was probably a rockfall or something. Don't worry about it, lover."

"A rockfall, eh? You're a trusting soul for a Molehiller."

"I'm just not as paranoid as an outsider like you."

The sound came again. The sound of someone walking with a limp, dragging a stiff leg over hard ground: step, *thump,* step, *thump,* step, *thump*.

It came from somewhere near, too.

"I suppose you don't hear that," Carstairs said.

"I hear it. So what?"

She tried to sound flip, but her voice was taut, strained.

He grabbed her wrist with his left hand and reached for his burner with his right. His hand closed over the grip, but he didn't pull the weapon.

"Hey, let go of my arm, you're hurting me!"

"I'd hate to fry your innards, but if this is some kind of a cross, that's just what I'll do."

"You crazy or something?!"

The limpster was very near now, on the other side of a fallen column. Suddenly the limping stopped.

Carstairs twisted Rima's arm behind her back, wedging her hand up between her shoulder blades. She cried out in pain. He stood her in front of him, a human shield. He drew his burner and jammed its blunt snout against her ribs, bruising them.

"If it's a trap you get it first, bitch!"

A head slowly rose into view above the top of the broken column. A man's head, pale, with wide staring eyes and an open mouth. Handsome, in a hard-bitten way, with a mass of curly hair elaborately styled in ringlets, a look currently in fashion with the dandified sugar pimps of the Gulch.

"Damon, look out! He's got a gun!"

Rima's warning ended in a squeal of agony as Carstairs twisted her arm harder.

"Friend of yours?" he said. "Tell him to come out and join the party."

"Damon, help me, please!"

Damon's expression remained unchanged. He didn't even blink, although his mouth gaped open as if he were shouting—a silent shout, since he made not a sound.

"Damon!"

Damon Pettigrew had been a successful Gulf Coast flesh peddler with a stable of high-priced whores, a sugar pimp who prided himself on motivating his women with seductive charm rather than terrorizing them into slavish submission. Of course, some girls wouldn't listen to sweet reason and required harsh discipline. He'd made the mistake of roughing up the wrong miss, a spitfire who rayed off his right leg at mid-thigh. He'd replaced it with an artificial limb, but the incident had affected his credibility and his whores had deserted him for other players.

Embittered and addicted, he wore out his welcome on the Coast and drifted inland, finally turning up in the Molehill Gulch. With little money and less local clout, he had no chance of plying his pimp's trade with a Syndicate sanction. He'd teamed up with Rima for a try at robbery and murder. She lured the johns to the ambush site, where he lay in wait to kill and rob them. The duo were small fish who'd thus far managed to escape the notice of the big boys, and the dead made no complaints.

The setup usually came off like clockwork, and that's why Rima couldn't believe that Damon had been stupid and clumsy enough to betray his presence and endanger them both.

"Come on out, friend. Nice and easy with no tricks, or the bitch gets burned down," Carstairs said.

Damon seemed to obey, but when he had shown himself to neck-height, he ran out of body. His severed head was stuck on the end of a pole being wielded by person or persons unknown, hiding behind the rocks.

Carstairs half grunted, half groaned. Rima choked back a cry, more of surprise than of anguish.

An eerie call split the night:

"Yi-yi-yi-yi-yi-yi-*yahoo!*"

The last tones of the mocking shriek died away.

"More friends of yours?" Carstairs said, digging the burner muzzle deeper into Rima's ribs.

Rima was tough and could take it. "They're no friends of mine or anyone else. They're Yahoos!"

As if in echo of her last word, the Yahoo war cry sounded again, coming this time from a different direction. Another howl rose up from a third unseen lurker, then a fourth, and a fifth.

"Christ, they're all around!" Carstairs said.

Damon's head on the pole bobbed up and down in accompaniment to the screaming chorus.

"You won't shoot me," Rima said. "You'll need every charge in the power cell to burn your way out of this!"

"I'll let them have you, that'll slow them down—"

Rima was a survival type with quick wits and quicker reflexes. While Carstairs was still speaking, she raised her right foot and brought it down hard, stomping the top of Carstairs's foot with her spiked heel, breaking bones.

Carstairs screamed in pain. Rima snapped her head back, butting him square in the face, pulping his nose. Carstairs staggered, loosening his grip on Rima's hand, which he was holding behind her back.

Pivoting on her left foot, Rima turned into him, shouldering him in the chest, knocking him even further off-balance. He jerked the trigger, but the burner muzzle was no longer in direct contact with her. A red ray lanced from the burner, searing across her side like a hot iron, carving a finger-sized furrow in her flesh.

A smell of burned meat filled the air, mixed with the acrid fumes of the cat suit, which had gone up in smoke. But Rima was lucky. It was only a grazing flesh wound, which had missed her vitals. There was next to no bleeding, since the heat ray had cauterized the wound even while inflicting it.

Rima threw herself to the side, breaking free from Carstairs's hold. He fell backward, sitting down hard. Rima dove, rolling behind a pile of rubble.

Blinking away tears of pain, Carstairs fired at her. The red ray splashed harmlessly against the rocks, vitrifying their surfaces. Carstairs stopped firing to conserve charge.

He rose to his knees, groaning, snuffling through his bloody nose. Rima was only about ten feet away, on the other side of the mound. There was no other cover in the immediate vicinity, and as soon as she showed herself, he'd burn her down. If she stayed, he'd just go around to the other side of the mound and get her there. It was very important to him to burn the bitch down.

She didn't have a weapon, as far as he could tell. Her skintight cat suit didn't leave any excess material for concealing even a small weapon, and his earlier gropings of her body hadn't turned up anything suspicious in that vein. Still, it wouldn't do to underestimate these Molehill guttersnipes; they were tricky.

Carstairs rose shakily, favoring his damaged right foot. It wasn't too bad as long as he kept most of his weight off it. That's what he thought until he took his first few stumbling steps forward. The pain made him grind his teeth. It would have been worse except that the injured area was starting to go numb. He'd get it fixed up fine once he was back in the walled city with its first-class medical facilities. That, and his broken nose, too. But not before he had settled the score with Rima.

No sign of the head on a pole or the Yahoos. The punks had probably taken it on the run when they saw he had a burner, gone off in search of easier, unarmed marks.

"Yi-yi-yi-yi-yi-*yahoo!*"

The war cry came from the darkness to his right. He crouched, swinging the burner in that direction to cover it. He heard movement, rubble crunching underfoot, but saw no one.

Something came sailing out from in front of him, striking him hard in the chest with a wet splattery squelch. He slipped but didn't fall. The object plopped to the ground at his feet.

It was Damon's head.

Carstairs freaked and fired without thinking. The red ray tore through the shadows from which the head had been pitched, painting the scene with ruby light. It was a wasted shot, since there was no one in view, although scurrying noises sounded beyond the red glare.

The ray wasn't as bright and tight as it had been, but there was still plenty of charge in the power cell. He'd have to be careful, though; he couldn't afford to waste any more shots. Maybe he'd be better off retreating while he still could. It galled him to let Rima escape, but he could always come back another time to take care of his unfinished business with her. For less than a half-day's salary, he could put a bounty on her head that would have half the hoodlums in the Gulch hunting for her. That was the smart way to play it.

Something whooshed past his head, coming so close that the wind of its passage lifted his hair—a rock, as big as two fists held together.

The next one didn't miss. It hit him in the thigh of his good leg, nearly knocking it out from under him. He hobbled around to keep from falling.

A flurry of rocks pelted him, accompanied by yipped yahooing. He raised his arms to protect his head. A big rock hit him in the back and he went down.

Agile forms popped up, breaking cover to rush him. Carstairs rayed the nearest, who was charging him head-down. The red ray cored the top of his skull and cooked his brains, killing him.

Another pounced from a different direction. Carstairs rayed him through the chest until the red light burned its way out of his back. That would have stopped a normal man, but the Yahoo kept coming, Aggro-potentiated and impervious to his mortal wound. Carstairs moved the ray to the side, cutting through the chest cavity into the heart. That was the killing stroke.

The Yahoo fell face-first, the fingers of his outstretched hands clawing the dirt inches from Carstairs.

The red ray was dark and cloudy; the burner's grip was warm to the touch.

Another Yahoo jumped him from behind, crashing down on his back, tearing at his throat, growling and snarling.

Carstairs rayed him in the face, which melted and bubbled away. He shrugged off the Yahoo, who thrashed around on the ground.

The burner was hot in his hand. The overheated power cell was on the verge of a meltdown.

Yahoos fenced him in on all sides, circling, surrounding him. They were just kids, kids who were hopped up on Aggro and foaming at the mouth to tear him apart.

Carstairs stuck the burner in his mouth, jammed the muzzle against the roof, and held down the trigger.

The ray cored his brain and blew out the top of his head.

The Yahoos fell on him, twenty or more, ripping and tearing, battering him with rocks, stabbing him with knives, gouging him with their bare hands, and even biting him. They vented their fury by rending his corpse.

A stinking haze of burnt flesh and boiled blood hung over the grisly scene.

A Yahoo filled his lungs deeply with the smell and smacked his lips.

"Hey—barbecue!" he said.

Rima lay on her belly and crawled away from the cannibal feast. Yahoos were scum at best, but this was a new high, or low, for them. Massive Aggro overdosing had stripped away one million years of hard-won evolution, regressing them into a pack of two-legged carnivores on a feeding frenzy.

How had they gotten hold of the massive amount of the drug needed to trigger this kind of reaction? The Yahoos barely had a pot to piss in, and the Maddogs would never have allowed their junior league more than a trickle of Aggro, for fear of just this result. At any rate, that was academic. The important question was, How was she going to get out of this alive?

She bellied into a ditch that angled away from the scene of the blood feast, into a mass of low mounds of dirt and stone. The feasters had forgotten about her in their frenzy.

She had gotten maybe a dozen yards away when a hand closed around her ankle.

A Yahoo squatted beside the ditch, hunkered down, with his eyes shining and his tongue hanging out. The tongue was purple and swollen to twice its normal size, another symptom of overdose.

He licked his lips, showing a mouthful of rotten teeth.

Rima rolled on her side, on top of the leg whose ankle he clutched, pulling him forward. His hand had a vise grip that didn't let go. Her free foot kicked him hard under the chin with the sharp pointed toe of her boot.

He grunted but didn't let go. She drove her spiked heel into the soft hollow of his throat, thrusting so hard that the impact tingled all the way up to her hip. The blow would have killed him under normal circumstances, if he hadn't been Aggro-dosed. As it was, it hurt him enough to make him let go.

He fell back, clutching his neck, gurgling, choking.

Rima got her feet under her, jumped up, and ran. She was as agile on high heels as the average individual was on flat-soled shoes, but the uneven terrain caused her to slow down.

A Yahoo loomed up in front of her, arms outspread, hands clenching and unclenching, eager to rip and rend and tear.

Rima reached behind her, grabbing the circlet anchoring the bottom of her ponytail and pulling it free. She flipped it at him with a twist of her wrist, as if she was skimming a pie plate.

The circlet was really a buzzbee, a lethal throwing weapon. When it left her hand, it activated, becoming a whirring saw-toothed blur, revolving at ultra-speed.

It hit the Yahoo in his middle and carved its way through his spine before running out of charge. He screamed and screamed as he was ripsawed in half, and after.

Now the alarm had been raised, and the Yahoos were after her in full force. Her eyes had long since grown accustomed to the dimness, and she could see that the slopes and hollows were crawling with the pack, maybe fifty or more who had been drawn by the commotion. And that wasn't counting the two dozen or so Yahoos who'd been snacking on Carstairs and were so much closer to her.

Rima jumped up on top of a fallen column and ran across it, nimble as a cat darting across the top of a fence.

A heat wave sizzled over her head, singeing the tips of her hair. A blood-red ray hissed through the air, fired from the burner that a Yahoo had pried from Carstairs's dead hand.

The column was broken into sections. Rima leaped from one to the next, making better time than she could have on the rubble-strewn ground.

The ray shot past her again, missing by an even wider margin, then fading into invisibility.

Its charge exhausted, while the firing mechanism was still engaged, the power cell suffered a meltdown. Anyone in his right mind would have let go of the scalding weapon, but not its Aggro-dosed wielder, who kept holding down the trigger, trying to make the burner work.

The metalloy housing turned to molten slag, burning his hand down to the bone. Like a school of sharks turning on their own in a fit of blood mania, other Yahoos went for the maimed gang member, dragging him down, tearing him apart.

But that was only a sideshow, a diversion from the main event, which was the taking of Rima. Baying like bloodhounds, most of the pack took out after her.

Narrowly avoiding the hands clutching at her legs, Rima jumped down to the other side of the column. One of her spiked heels broke off in the fall. She paused long enough to try to knock the other one loose against a paving stone. She'd run faster without the heels, but she wouldn't get very far without the boots, not on this jagged ground. The heel was partially dislodged. She grabbed it and pulled it off the rest of the way. Tiny bent nails protruded from the heel.

A Yahoo came scrambling over the top of the column and lunged at her. She stepped inside his arms and rammed the heel nails-first into the bridge of his nose, shattering the bone there and driving the splinters into his brain.

He fell back, dead, but two more came over the top. She turned and ran, fighting down panic as she heard more and more Yahoos hop the column and take up the chase.

The ground sloped upward. The base of the slope was covered with loose dirt and grit that was treacherous underfoot. Jutting out of the ridge at an acute angle was a titanic slab of masonry, a section of collapsed roadway. Here, footing was more secure. She scrambled to the top of the slab, having nowhere else to go.

Empty space loomed before her as she reached the jagged lip of the slab. Yahoos were right behind her.

Rima threw herself into empty air, not knowing what lay below and not caring. Whatever it was, it couldn't be as bad as the Yahoos. Even a broken neck would be better than being taken alive by them.

A breathless instant followed, of falling through space into darkness, her mind empty of everything but the sensation of plunging. A long drop, and then the ground rose up, slamming into her.

It was loose dirt, not solid ground, but it still fetched her a tremendous blow. She was on a long, steep incline, tumbling head over heels, bouncing, sliding, unable to stop her fall.

Then she pitched forward and smacked hard ground, a level surface that stopped her battering descent.

She saw stars. She was scraped and bruised and numb on one side.

Yipping yahoo howls cut through her stunned stupor, prodding her into motion. *Keep moving, don't stop,* she thought, even though flight seemed hopeless. She breathed a silent prayer to her own private god-devils: *Let me live and I'll be good from now on, I swear it!*

She had trouble focusing her eyes. She was in a pit of darkness. The yowling came from behind her, so she crawled forward on her hands and knees.

The pit rang with echoing shrieks. The hard ground vibrated with many footfalls closing in on her.

A shape loomed up ahead, darker than the darkness. It had hard edges, slanting surfaces. Wan moonlight filtered down through a rift in the clouds, outlining the object.

It was a machine of some sort, probably some long-abandoned piece of construction or earth-moving equipment left in a crater to rust away. Maybe she could crawl under it and hide, or at least find some sharp edge to cut her throat on before the Yahoos got her.

Too late. They were almost upon her, the leaders of the pack so close she could feel the body heat wafting off them.

And then the machine came to life.

SEVEN

APU-805 MUSTERED ITS last reserves for a final go-round.

Autonomic patrol unit #805, Scout series model Bird Dog, prepared to clash with the Yahoos. Bird Dog versus the junior auxiliary league of the Maddog Posse. It was as good a way to die as any and better than most.

And Bird Dog could die. More than a machine, it was a crime-busting mechanism with a human personality at its core. A conscious entity aware of its own mortality. Its mission: protect the innocent and pulverize the guilty.

Of course, Rima was hardly an innocent, but Bird Dog didn't know that, and it wouldn't have made any difference if it had known. Bird Dog would have reacted the same way even if she were the wickedest woman in the world. She was running for her life from a mob that meant to take it. That was all Bird Dog needed to know. Besides, the human whose personality had been impressed on its cybernetic brain was the chivalrous type, so that was a factor, too.

Not only was Bird Dog near the end of its existence, but it was one of the last of its kind, its kind being the APU class of self-guiding mobile machinery built in Texas to quell the anarchic violence following the Last War. The numerical designation 805 did not mean that it was the eight-hundred-and-fifth such unit to enter active duty; rather, that it was the fifth model of the series 8 Scout/Bird

Dog type. Less than fifty of the entire APU class had ever been commissioned, and of those, the majority fell in the higher-numbered, more compact light armored vehicle series, such as the Scout/Bird Dog. Only a relative handful of the low-numbered Juggernaut, Blockbuster, and Battle Wagon series had been put out in the field, and they were the first to be retired. The Last War had been over a quarter-century ago (the last big one, that is; there had been nothing but small wars ever since), and by A.D. 2035 only a few of the smallest models had managed to avoid recall.

Such a one was Bird Dog.

Its primary mission was the detection, confiscation, and/or destruction of illegal E-weps (energy weapons), along with those who disseminated same. Bomb disposal was another priority, what with all the unexploded antipersonnel devices, booby traps, and smart mines that the enemy Red Chinese and their allies had sowed throughout the state during the war (throughout much of the nation, too). But Bird Dog's secondary responsibilities encompassed the entire spectrum of law enforcement activities.

The pursuit of its prime mission had brought Bird Dog to Molehill. Coming by night to the wasteland, it arrived unseen. It had been idling in its passive mode, seeking traces of the high-energy signature of the prohibited E-weps it had been trailing. It sheltered in a hollow a hundred feet below the north edge of the collapsed overpass, its passive sensors scanning the EMG spectrum.

Then came Rima. When she threw herself off the top of the rubble ridge, the long slope of loose dirt and ashes on the other side had cushioned her falling slide so she received nothing worse than a battering and a partial skinning on her way down to the bottom of the pit.

Her proximity to Bird Dog activated its bio-sensors. Her distress was evident: rapid heartbeat and respiratory rate, venting of fear pheromones, and atypical cooling of the outer skin areas were all symptoms of the primal flight-or-fight syndrome.

The Yahoo horde swarming down into the pit defined the situation. Bird Dog knew a kill-crazy mob when it saw one. In the last twenty years it had seen and handled many such mobs.

Problem analyzed, action was indicated and initiated. Bird Dog switched from passive to active mode.

What Rima had thought was an abandoned wreck came to life.

Bird Dog was an armored box on wheels. Six wheels now—two of its original eight-wheel configuration were beyond repair. Its front glacis plate was tilted at a 45-degree angle to minimize the impact of antiarmor weapons. It was fifteen feet long with an eight foot wheel base, its edges streamlined and its exterior smoothly unbroken for radar-foiling stealth. It was low to the ground to present a minimal target. It looked like a low-slung chisel on wheels.

The ruined old highway served as the present-day air transportation corridor for the big freightliner caravans making the run to Mountain. The crash site where the Yahoos had scavenged the Aggro was about a mile away from the pit where Bird Dog sat. About three hundred overdosed gangbangers had been making their erratic way across the wasteland since nightfall, drawn by the lights of the Gulch. Linear progress wasn't their strong suit, so it had taken them hours to get nowhere fast. The urban wasteland wasn't empty; there had been plenty of bums, dipsos, dope fiends, hermits, homeless families, and other lost souls to butcher.

The leading edge of the pack had encountered Damon Pettigrew while he was lurking in wait for Rima to return with her john. They killed him and decided to use the body parts to have some fun with the new arrivals. The fun turned out to be livelier than expected when Carstairs cut loose with the burner and Rima ran for her life.

Violence draws Aggros like flies to fresh manure. When Rima tumbled into the pit, a hundred Yahoos more or less were baying at her heels in hot pursuit.

Bird Dog came alive. It's a toss-up as to who was more surprised, Rima or the Yahoos.

The patrol vehicle shuddered as its engines switched on. The noise wasn't loud, just a deep vibratory thrumming that was as much felt as heard. The driving motor was rigged with sound-suppressing baffles and other devices to ensure that it ran as quietly as possible. An underlying whooshing sound was the high-speed injectors feeding the engines an enriched blend of converted hydrogen fuel for peak performance. Power cells transformed hot exhaust gases into usable energy for other machine functions, a fuel-saving design that also helped minimize the vehicle's telltale infrared heat signature.

Bird Dog's dwindling reserves of ammo, power, and spare parts worked against the Yahoos. Standard operating procedure called for non-lethal methods of riot control, if possible. *If possible.* That was the escape clause. Bird Dog's store of vom-gas and convulsion fog cannisters was exhausted. Its hyper- and sub-sonic generator was long defunct. Precious power could not be wasted charging the electric-arc shock beamer.

The six-barrel rotary Gatling-style turret gun was still operational, though.

The turret was shaped like a cigarette box laid on its side. A shutter was retracted in a recessed vent in the center of the armor plate in front, opening the gun port. A short stubby gun was thrust out about three feet or so, its barrel having six blackened metalloy tubes grouped around a central axis.

Bird Dog was out of baton rounds, too, the so-called "rubber bullets" that were often useful in dispersing crowds in situations where fatalities were not desirable. Rubber bullets wouldn't have stopped the Yahoos.

Some rounds of live ammunition were available.

"HALT!"

Condensor-grid vobox exterior speakers broadcast Bird Dog's command at high volume. Echoes rippled to the lip of the pit and beyond.

Public relations concerns had prompted a misguided attempt to personalize the APU class with human speaking voices. A wasted effort, since the average citizen was scared like hell of the machines, and there was no way for the makers to put a positive spin on that. Bird Dog's voice reproduced the flat, bored, reedy tones of the squad car dispatcher whose voice had been digitally sampled to provide the vocal template, a benumbed individual who sounded more machinelike than any speaking machine.

"CEASE AND DESIST YOUR ILLEGAL ACTIVITIES OR FIRING WILL COMMENCE."

It is doubtful whether the Yahoos would have understood the carefully phrased legal-speak of the ultimatum even if they had been in their right minds, such as they were. Aggrodosed, it affected them not at all, except to further inflame them.

"Hey, yo! Somebody's in that tin can!"

"Peel open that piece of shit and then peel open the driver!"

They were young and knew nothing of APUs. Not a story or even a word about the Last War and its aftermath had ever reached them; if it had, they would have ignored it. They were without history.

Many were without lives, after Bird Dog opened fire.

A warning had been broadcast. Scant ammunition must not be expended on the luxury of a volley of warning shots.

Bird Dog started blasting. Rima lay huddled on the ground, well below the line of fire. The rotary gun barrel spun on its own axis, spitting out slugs so fast that the muzzle flares from six separate bores seemed to become a solid ring of fire.

Some of those at the head of the chase were so close to Rima that the rotary gun caught them at point-blank range when it opened up. The damage was frightful.

Computerized fire control made every shot count. One shot, one kill, that's all it took, even for drug-crazed runamucks like the Yahoos. The slugs were moving so fast that even if they struck an arm or leg the massive hydrostatic pressure would kill on impact.

A fan of dead bodies spread across the floor of the pit and started to climb the opposite side. The point of the fan was a corpse sprawled a few feet away from Bird Dog. Behind it lay two more corpses, and behind them, four; behind that four lay eight and so on, to the lower slopes of the pit wall.

It was a massacre, but the vehicle's makers hadn't been particularly tenderhearted about murderous mobs. Rough justice was required to stem the chaotic aftermath of the Last War.

Shooting stopped. Disengaged, the rotary gun wound down, its shrill mosquito whine dropping into a low bass tone.

There were still plenty more Yahoos left on the upper slopes, and the main body of the gang was massed still farther beyond, atop the wrecked old highway, but Bird Dog lacked the wherewithal to handle them. Besides, that would be overkill, since enough of the assailants had been eliminated to allow the unit to secure its immediate objective—namely, protecting the person of the pursued.

A starboard side port opened, and an extensible mek-arm extruded. A hatch opened in the top of the vehicle, just before the front edge of the turret, disclosing a large square-shaped compartment.

Rima had been frozen in place during the shooting, but when the mek-arm started reaching for her, she moved. Not fast enough—the grippers at the business end of the prosthesis closed around her ankle.

The grippers were strong enough to bend metalloy beams yet delicate enough to pick up an egg without cracking it. They picked up Rima, lifting her upside-down and hoisting her above the open hatchway. She screamed, then decided against it as a waste of breath. She squirmed and fought and struggled in vain to break free.

The mek-arm gently but firmly lowered her head-first into an unlit compartment. Its sides and floor were padded. The hatch swung shut, sealing her into the dark box. The underside of the hatch was padded, too. There was room enough to sit up but not to lie down.

Rima felt as if she'd been locked into a coffin. She screamed.

Glo-buttons embedded in the walls came on, shedding a pearly light.

"YOU HAVE BEEN TAKEN INTO PROTECTIVE CUSTODY SOLELY TO PRESERVE YOUR PERSONAL SAFETY," a voice said from a hidden speaker.

Rima jumped, hitting her head on the padded ceiling.

"YOU WILL BE RELEASED AS SOON AS THE IMMEDIATE THREAT IS ENDED. IN THE MEANTIME, FRESH AIR IS BEING SUPPLIED TO YOU AND WILL CONTINUE TO BE SUPPLIED FOR THE DURATION OF THE CURRENT EMERGENCY."

Canned air, not fresh. Rima could taste the rubber-tinged staleness of air from a tank. It came hissing in from an unseen vent somewhere in the box.

"THE STATE OF TEXAS REGRETS ANY INCONVENIENCE YOU MAY HAVE SUFFERED, BUT HEREBY INFORMS YOU THAT IT IS INDEMNIFIED AGAINST ANY DAMAGES, LAWSUITS, OR CIVIL COURT ACTIONS RESULTING FROM THE PRESENT INTERVENTION, AS SPECIFIED IN THE APPROPRIATE STATUTES IN THE POSTWAR RECOVERY ACT SIGNED INTO LAW ON AUGUST 20, A.D. 2016, DETAILS PROVIDED UPON WRITTEN REQUEST."

"Are you kidding? Listen, just who in the fuck *are* you?" Rima said.

"APU #805, SCOUT SERIES MODEL BIRD DOG."

"You talk like a robot or something. Is that what you are?"

"NEGATIVE."

"Whew, that's a relief! Those things scare the shit out of me."

"ROBOTS ARE OTHER-DIRECTED. THIS UNIT IS AUTONOMIC. SELF-GUIDED."

"Shit, then you are a machine!"

"YES AND NO."

"Huh? What does that mean? You man or machine or what?"

"YES."

"Yes, you're a man? Or, yes, you're a machine?"

"OR WHAT. NEITHER MAN NOR MACHINE, THIS UNIT IS, AS YOU PUT IT, AN 'OR-WHAT.' "

"You're scaring me. Don't do that."

"DELIGHTFUL CHATTING WITH YOU, BUT MUST NOW CLOSE DOWN COMMUNICATION TO ATTEND TO OTHER DUTIES."

"Hey, wait—"

The Yahoos at the top of the pit had sufficiently recovered from the shock to return fire. Mostly they were armed with simple ballistic weapons: auto-guns, mini-machine pistols, wheel guns, sawed-off wheel shotguns. No energy weapons that were any good. Kid stuff.

Low-velocity slugs rained down on Bird Dog, splashing harmlessly against its armor. Mek-arm and rotary gun withdrew into their respective niches; hatches and ports sealed themselves shut.

Bird Dog followed a hierarchical pyramid of priorities. At the apex was its prime mission, the neutralization of illegal energy weapons and their operators. Below that was the great bulk of more routine peacekeeping functions, the secondary law-and-order components of its mission, such as protecting life and property. It could perform its secondary duties so long as they did not conflict with achieving the long-range goals of its prime mission. It had done so when it rescued Rima. Its plan now was to take the girl (and itself) safely out of the danger zone, release her, and resume its search for the illicit E-weps, which had brought it to Molehill in the first place.

A human wave of latecoming Yahoos slopped down over the lip of the pit and began pouring down the slope. Those who had managed to hold onto their guns, despite the Aggro mania, used them. Gunfire crackled; gunsmoke shrouded the upper regions of the pit like a low-hanging cloud.

Bird Dog went into reverse, its powerful engine turning each of the independently mounted six wheels left to it. The oversized tires were solid body composition, bulletproof but hard to replace. Bird Dog couldn't just roll up to a repair shop to have the tires changed, since it was in a sense a rogue unit, having avoided recall and retirement. It did not consider itself an outlaw, since it did not recognize the authority of the agency seeking to mothball the APUs. It did its own repairs, and what it couldn't fix it cannibalized for spare parts.

Big wheels kicked up dust as Bird Dog began its retreat. Bullets spanged and spattered against it, with the heavier-caliber slugs pelting it like hailstones. Jouncing, bumping, and lurching, it made its way toward the north side of the pit.

Its retreat whipped the Yahoos to a new peak of frenzy. They had it on the run, but it mustn't escape to cheat them of their victory. They ran after it, some sliding down the south slope to the pit floor, others fanning out across the top of the east and west walls. More than a few broke bones in their wild descent, ignored the injuries, and hobbled, hopped, or crawled to continue the chase. Some of the Aggro-dosed were so excited by the racket of gunfire that they shot their fellows for the thrill of seeing them die. Gunfights and savage hand-to-hand combats flared up, violent eddies in the torrent of madness.

Bird Dog plowed across the rugged terrain of the pit floor, which was cracked and cratered like the surface of the moon. The vehicle was dark, needing no visible-spectrum headlights to find its path, since its sensors used infrared imagers to make the night as clear as daylight on its internal guidance screens.

It took the low ground, weaving between dunes, dirt mounds, and rock piles. The pit floor narrowed toward the north, where a gap in the wall opened onto broad, sprawling flatlands. Once it was on the flat, Bird Dog could quickly outdistance its pursuers. They were gaining on it in the pit, though, since they could go in a straight line over hills and hummocks the vehicle had to swing wide detours around.

Some of the Yahoos had kept their heads, those who had come late to the Aggro orgy and had to take the leavings of the drug. They steered clear of the mad stampede of the drug-deranged. One such Yahoo had a chopped carbine loaded with explosive bullets. He ran along the west lip of the pit, angling for a clear shot at the vehicle.

Bird Dog wound through a group of mounds whose tops were taller than its turret. That provided some cover, but the plume of dust churned up in its wake was a ghostly signpost betraying its position.

Snugging the butt of the shortened stock to his shoulder, the carbineer pointed his weapon at the head of the plume. The thin red line of a laser target-finder probed through the murk, fingering the dull graphite-black finish of the patrol vehicle. He fired, missed. The explosive bullet blew the top off a dirt mound.

The hummocks rose higher still as Bird Dog went deeper into them, screening itself from further shots for the moment.

The carbineer ran toward the far end of the pit, leaping from rock to rock like a gazelle, scrambling to reach his goal before the vehicle broke through into open ground. Negotiating the S-curves through the dunes slowed Bird Dog.

The carbineer clambered up a massive flat-topped rock at the northwest rim, near the brink of the gap in the wall. A good vantage point for a sniper. He had beaten Bird Dog to the gap, too.

Assuming a prone position facing south, he lined up his laser sights on the long, flat open ground between the dunes and the rift.

BIRD DOG emerged from the saddle between two mounds. The carbine's target-finding red line pinlighted the emerging vehicle.

Sensors instantly alerted the unit that it was being ranged, but there was no room for evasive maneuvering. Burners or beamers would have negated the threat, but the power cells were too weak to charge the energy weapons. There was neither room enough nor time to swing the turret around to bring the rotary gun into play, since it had been covering the rear during the retreat.

BIRD DOG shifted into high gear, pouring on a burst of speed. It seemed to catapult into the open, wheels grooving deep ruts in the earth.

The sniper fired, overshooting the mark with his first round. Dirt and smoke spouted upward where the explosive bullet struck.

Correcting his aim, he led the target, sighting in advance of the oncoming vehicle. The shot scored, striking square on the slanted glacis plate.

There was a *whooming* sound, a ringing concussion of piledriver impact. But that was where the armor plate was thickest, and its tilted angle deflected much of the force. It was a hit, though, and the vehicle seemed to shrink as the massive shock absorbers of its heavy-duty suspension system recoiled under the blow.

The vehicle nosed down, pancaked on its underside, shivered, shook off the hit and kept on going.

A long, narrow hatch on the port side opened and out popped a .50-caliber machine gun, gimbal-mounted at the end of a short, stubby mek-arm—a heavy machine gun, technically, but small arms compared to the rotary gun. The muzzle swung outward and up, using the sniper's laser target-finder as a guide to sight in on him.

Reflexes sharpened to razor keenness by Aggro, he spotted the movement and rolled clear of the stream of slugs that came blasting at him. He was protected by the rocky overhang of his perch.

Squeezing off rapid-fire bursts to keep him pinned down, the vehicle raced for the gap. But the .50 ammunition ran out first.

The sniper poked the muzzle of his weapon over the cliff edge just as Bird Dog presented a broadside target as it entered the mouth of the gap. The round tagged it in the middle of the portside wheel well.

The blast lifted that side a few feet off the ground, so for a span of time the vehicle was riding on the three wheels of the opposite side.

"UGH!"

That sound coming across the speaker grid jolted Rima

worse than the pounding she'd been taking during the wild retreat. She'd never heard a machine grunt before, but she knew it was not a good sign.

Bird Dog righted itself, wobbled, and fishtailed in the pass, fighting to regain control. The portside center wheel was crippled. The internal guidance system cut power to the drive shaft, putting the wheel out of commission, while the remaining wheels on both sides automatically compensated to adjust to its loss.

The damaged wheel base tore loose from its axle moorings but failed to break off completely. Whipsawing from side to side, it hammered against the wheels bracketing it, pounding them with brutal blows, further confounding the vehicle's precarious balance.

The unit rushed toward a rock wall at an oblique angle. It detonated explosive bolts, blowing the damaged wheel clear of the vehicle, but too late.

Bird Dog swerved to avoid a collision and might have made it if not for a rocky outcropping that thrust away from the rift wall. The vehicle struck it with its right front, slewed around, and slammed its starboard side smack against the stones.

It came to a halt, gears grinding, wheels spinning.

This was far from a mortal blow to a vehicle that was designed to survive a direct hit from an artillery shell or beamer blast. Indeed, the rocks were shattered at the point of impact, while the armored shell was hardly dented. But the front end was partially buried under a mass of crushed stone fragments, most of them the size of bowling balls, and fist-sized chunks carpeted the ground at the crash site, clogging the wheel wells and making it difficult for the tires to find much traction.

The sniper had a brainstorm. Instead of shooting at the armored car, he fired at a stone ledge overhanging it some twenty feet above the ground.

Thumbing the selector to auto-fire, he held down the trigger, emptying the clip into the rocky abutment. A fusillade of explosive bullets hammered the stones, blasting big slabs loose from the cliff. A mini-avalanche resulted, heaping boulders on the vehicle, immobilizing it.

The Yahoos arrived in force a moment later. There was no need to rush; Bird Dog wasn't going anywhere in the near future, not until it dug itself out of a couple of tons of earth and stone. The Yahoos could shell it at their leisure, to get at the meat inside.

So they thought.

EIGHT

RIMA FELT AS if she had gone over the falls in a barrel while being mugged by a giant killer pillow at the same time.

The pillow was still in her face, literally, and all over the rest of her, too. It was an inflatable safety air bag which had erupted from what looked like a rivet in the wall, expanding to fill the compartment in a few seconds when Bird Dog began its retreat. Engulfing Rima, the protective device swaddled her from head to toe in a seamless cocoon, infinitely yielding but unbreakable. A fold of it kept pressing against her nose, forcing her to turn her head to the side in order to breath. The material gave off a thick stale synthetic scent.

The air bag combined with the padded inner compartment to cushion her against the battering she otherwise would have gotten from Bird Dog's wild dash for the gap. It buffered the pressure waves from explosive rounds impacting the vehicle. The concussion from the hit that destroyed the wheel squeezed Rima like a giant invisible hand. It gave her a nosebleed and she almost threw up. That wasn't too pleasant, not with the air bag's doughy folds hugging her.

The collision with the cliff wall wasn't as bad as the explosive bullets, but the rockfall which followed hard upon it was worse than either. At one point, the air bag pressed Rima flat against the floor, so hard that she feared that the roof of the vehicle had collapsed. The crushing pressure ceased when the rocks stopped falling.

"Drive much?" Rima said.

Her voice sounded thin and strained to her in the hush that followed the avalanche. It was hard to talk with the air bag pressing against her jaws, chest, and diaphragm.

There was no reply.

"What the fuck happened?!"

She feared that the cybernetic brain was down, its vital spark of awareness extinguished, entombing her in an inert, armored coffin. At that, it was still a better way to go than being torn apart by Yahoos. But it was a bitter blow, bitter. For a moment she had dared to hope that she might actually get out of this with a whole skin.

Glo-buttons shone on uninterruptedly, providing her with some cold comfort that the machinery hadn't quit completely.

"PLEASE STAND BY."

Rima gasped thanks that Bird Dog hadn't been wiped from existence. She would have made the holy sign too, if the air bag hadn't been straitjacketing her limbs. Funny how a person reaches for that old-time religion in a jam, she thought.

"THIS UNIT IS EXPERIENCING TECHNICAL DIFFICULTIES. PLEASE STAND BY."

"We've stopped. We're not moving, I can feel it!"

"PROGRESS HAS BEEN TEMPORARILY DELAYED. MOVEMENT WILL RESUME AS SOON AS POSSIBLE."

"How soon is that?"

"THE STATE OF TEXAS REGRETS ANY INCONVENIENCE THAT THE DELAY MAY CAUSE YOU, WITH THE STIPULATION THAT SAID REGRETS DO NOT IMPLY ANY ACKNOWLEDGEMENT OF LIABILITY FOR ANY INJURIES OR LOSS RESULTING FROM SAID DELAY."

"That bad, huh? What happened? It sounded like a mountain fell on us."

Bird Dog made no reply.

"We're stuck," Rima said.

"TEMPORARILY."

"Yeah, well, here's where I get off. Thanks for the ride; it's been nice knowing you. Now take this overgrown marshmallow off of me and let me out of here!"

"PLEASE STAND BY."

The patrol vehicle was half-buried, but that didn't stop the Yahoos from firing at the half that wasn't. Grouped in an arc facing it, gang gunners unloaded their weapons at the armored car's exposed rear. The storm of slugs succeeded only in inflicting cosmetic damage, scratching the composite armor plates and bouncing off the back tires. Ricochets killed six and wounded twice that before the firing ceased. Vulnerability brings out the worst in Aggro maniacs. The most toxically deranged users fell on the wounded, making cruel sport of their screaming sufferings. Other Yahoos then slaughtered the slaughterers, adding greatly to the fun.

A hardcore element focused their attention on the armored car.

"Gonna be a tough nut to crack," a gangbanger said.

"Bombs! That'll do it," another said.

"Great. You got any?"

"No."

"Know where to get some?"

"Well, no—"

"Then what'd you bring it up for, you dumb son of a bitch?"

The other Yahoo pulled a knife and lunged, but the first speaker had already drawn his gun. He shot the knife-wielder in the forehead.

"Dumb motherfucker," he said, chuckling.

A blast struck down from above, blowing him to bits— an explosive bullet, fired by the sniper on top of the cliff, who had done it just for a gag.

A handful of bystanders who had been caught in the blast area were messed up pretty bad. Others shot back at the sniper, who had already gone to cover. He lay on his back laughing as the return fire zipped harmlessly past him.

A rift opened in the clouds, baring a swatch of starry sky. Suddenly a shape deeper than the darkness passed across the stars, blotting them from view. A torpedo shape, a sky shark.

The sniper sat up, startled, rubbing his eyes, craning for another glimpse of the apparition. Bullets from below whizzed close by his head, forcing him to flatten out of range.

When he looked again, the shark shape was gone, nowhere to be seen, hidden perhaps behind a cloud. If it had ever existed at all, and wasn't just a hallucination. But he had taken a light dose of Aggro, a body drug not known for producing hallucinations.

Leader types among the Yahoos had generally taken less Aggro than their fellows, in order to keep on top of the situation. Control was their drug of choice. Banding together, they bullied a large number of less-focused individuals into doing their bidding, which meant making a coordinated attack on the armored car. Some of the crazies were gunned down to show that the chiefs meant business. The message got across, chilling the crowd.

The rock slide had trapped the vehicle so that its forward and middle wheels were so smothered in stones that they were unable to move. The APU was tilted nose-down, raising the rear wheels off the ground with nothing to get a grip on but empty air. The turret with its terrible rotary gun and the side-mounted machine gun were rendered useless by the ton or two of medicine ball–sized boulders piled on them.

A rear top hatch opened and a mek-arm popped out, panicking the Yahoos into another volley of gunfire. Shooting echoed from wall to wall in the gap, filling the notch with noise.

The elongated mek-arm looked like the spindly limb of some gigantic metal insect. With precise, delicate movements, it fastened its clawlike grippers on a football-sized stone, plucking it from the pile on top of the vehicle and tossing it aside. It reached for another stone and repeated the process.

At that rate it might succeed in digging itself out in a day or two, provided it wasn't stymied by the big boulders.

A squat, square-shaped Yahoo fired a wheel auto-shotgun at the vehicle, from close range. He was strong and solid enough to fire it on auto without the recoil knocking him flat on his ass.

Three of the loads were bombshell rounds. They hammered the mek-arm. When the smoke cleared, the mek-arm was twisted, blackened, bent at odd angles. Struts and cables curled off the main shaft like broken guitar strings. It tried to retract into its compartment but too many joints had been broken for it to fold up and fit into the niche. It hung drooping and flapping, a pathetic sight.

Another genius was inspired to jump on the back of the vehicle and empty his handgun into the open mek-arm compartment, to no effect.

That started a general rush toward the trapped unit. Aggro users crave violent action, even if it's something as primitive as banging a rock against an armor-plated APU. A dozen or so of them piled onto the patrol car to do just that.

They were active and noisy. It was the closest most of them had ever come to anything resembling real work. If they kept it up for a year or two, they might begin to make a dent in the composite armor shell.

Stuck hanging in midair, the rear wheels seemed vulnerable. Wrecking groups went to work on them, pounding the axles and support struts where they joined the wheel bases.

Yahoos swarmed over the prowler like soldier ants trying to deconstruct a downed scorpion. But the prowler could still sting.

Without warning, Bird Dog applied power to the rear drive shafts, going from zero RPMs to a speed of sixty miles per hour.

Whirling wheels pureed the wreckers.

The crippled mek-arm began to flail about, scything the Yahoos on the vehicle. Spines snapped, skulls were smashed, and some of the casualties were brushed off into the path of the spinning wheels.

Mek-arm and wheels stopped cold the instant that the last available victim had been taken care of.

The rank-and-file gangbangers predictably went off on another futile shooting spree. This time, the leaders were able to quell it quickly.

A wide-awake type had noticed that the mek-arm, while deadly, was so damaged that it could only operate within a fairly limited arc of movement. An attack launched from outside those limits had every chance of success.

The tactic was put into motion. Thirty strongbacks, divided into two groups, climbed the rock pile on both sides of the prowler, using it as a stairway to mount the top of the vehicle and approach the mek-arm from its unprotected rear. All were careful to steer clear of the mek-arm's reach and the now-inert wheels.

The prosthesis seesawed, stymied by its inability to reach behind itself.

The Yahoos rushed it, piling on top of it, pinning it down by sheer weight of numbers. They fought it like circus roustabouts wrestling a giant python into center ring.

They were on the verge of winning when Bird Dog initiated a new self-defense ploy. Its outer shell became electrified. It was like switching on a giant bug-zapper. Cooked Yahoos went up in smoke, their dark forms dwindling at the heart of the discharge's dazzling glare.

Bird Dog de-electrified. Charge hung heavy in the air, snapping and sparking. Charred remains smoldered.

"That damn machine is making a monkey out of us!" somebody said at last.

There were no disagreements.

The Yahoos had bitten off more than they could chew. Their numbers had dropped from an original three hundred plus to less than a third of that. Making war on the Prowler was too much like work. It wasn't fun. Some on the periphery of the scene began moving away into the darkness, in search of easier pickings.

Industrial-strength burners, plasmatic chainsaws, and demolition pile drivers would be needed to crack Bird Dog's shell. They could be had, but not tonight. It was a point of honor that the prowler must be destroyed. No man, no machine, could put this kind of hurting on the

Yahoos and get away with it. Such a humiliating defeat would destroy their credibility on the street, and that would be the end of all of them.

So agreed the gang chieftains, who were huddling to brainstorm a plan. They finally decided to say the hell with it tonight and come back tomorrow to do the job right. It was highly unlikely that the prowler would have freed itself by then. It was much more likely that some rival gang would happen by and take a crack at it. The prowler was potential wealth, a fortune in weapons, computer components, spare parts.

"Don't forget the Maddogs. They'll claim it for themselves since it's on their turf," somebody said.

"Sure, after we break our backs doing the dirty work."

"Like always."

"Shit, they'll be pissed that nobody even passed the word about it to them."

"They'll be pissed about us holding out on the Aggro, too."

"I don't know about you, but me, I didn't hold out nothing on nobody. Somebody gave me a taste of the stuff and I took it and that's all I know."

"Try telling that to the Dogs and see what it gets you. They'll cut your ass off."

"Yours, too!"

"All our asses, unless we can figure a way out."

"If we get hold of that rotary gun, we'll be the Maddogs."

The other chieftains all turned to look at this last speaker. Meneer, his name was.

"Well, why not? With a wep like that, we could kick ass, instead of getting our asses kicked, which is what's gonna happen if we don't get us some heavy firepower," he said.

"You could get dead just for saying that, Meneer."

"Yeah? And you all could get dead just for hearing it. You want to be suckers all your lives?—Which won't be long, considering."

"Big talk, but we're a long way off from cracking that hellbox on wheels, in case you haven't noticed."

"Shut up, Lutie. Meneer's got a plan."

"Don't tell me to shut up, Kharg, or I'll—*Ugh!*"

Lutie's torso bowed outward as he was stabbed in the back. Life went out of him, but he stayed on his feet until the knife-wielder pulled out his blade.

"Nice work, Cholla."

"Thanks, Kharg."

Cholla wiped the blade clean on his pants leg before sheathing it. "What's the plan?"

"Ever hear of buried treasure? That's what we're gonna do. The machine's already half-buried. We'll finish the job, cover it up with a couple more tons of rock for safekeeping. Bury it deep enough and nobody'll know that it's there. We come back later with the right tools and dig it up," Meneer said.

"What happens when one of our boys shoots his mouth off? Or the Dogs grab some of our guys and start putting on the pressure for some answers? They'll spill their guts in a second, and so would I, once the torturers start in on you."

"Dead men tell no tales, Joe."

"*What?!* You don't mean that we should blip the rest of the guys?"

"Why not?" Meneer said, shrugging.

"They're our brothers!"

"Tell it to the birds."

"There's some good dudes out there. Friends of mine," Cholla said.

"Yeah! Plus, the eight of us might have trouble blipping a hundred of them," Viceroy said.

He was pale, puffy-faced, sullen, with restless slitted eyes.

"We're going to need all the good guns we can get, with the Dogs on our trail," said Boyking, Viceroy's partner.

"Okay, we keep the reliables and blip everybody else," Meneer said.

"I'll buy that," Joe said, seeming relieved.

"We can always get rid of them later," Meneer added.

Faucon was horse-faced, with thick black brows that looked phony but weren't. He glanced over his shoulder at the main body of Yahoos, who were out of earshot.

"If they could hear us now they'd tear our hearts out," he said.

"They'd cross us if they could but we thought of it first. Hell, the whole gang is living on borrowed time anyway."

"How do you figure that, Meneer?"

"We signed our death warrants when we dragged down the Aggro instead of bucking it up the line to the Dogs."

"They wouldn't blip everybody!"

"No, just the guys that the machine missed."

"They couldn't get away with that."

"You're a trusting soul, Joe. Nobody'd squawk if we turned up dead. Most folks'd say 'good riddance.' And maybe you think there aren't a thousand snot-noses who'd rush in to take our place stooging for the big boys? I tell you, we're as good as dead unless we crack that hellbox and grab the goodies. With them, we can blip the Dogs and be the new kings of the hill," Meneer said.

"I'm sold," Kharg said.

The other chieftains—Cholla, Viceroy, Boyking, Joe, Rakeesh, Bliss, and Faucon—agreed to go along with Meneer's scheme. If they had any doubts or misgivings, they kept them to themselves. Besides, even a light dose of Aggro, such as they had taken, made the user feel invulnerable, unstoppable.

"First we bury the hellbox good and deep, then we blip whoever looks like they can't cut it. Anybody comes along to investigate, all they'll find is a bunch of stiffs left over from an Aggromaniac murder orgy. The Dogs will lighten up when they see that most of the membership is dead. They'll figure that they can hunt down the survivors in their own sweet time. That'll buy us some time to make moves," Meneer said.

"Wonder why the Dogs haven't shown up already to check things out," Rakeesh said.

"Because they're lazy bastards. Because they're too busy sucking up to the big-time operators to take care of business. And mainly because a bunch of real crazies split off from the rest of our gang early to go raise hell in the Gulch. The Dogs'll have their hands full cleaning up on those maniacs."

"Best not push our luck. Let's do what we got to do and clear out fast," Kharg said.

"We need tools for when we come back," Faucon said.

"I know some guys who do body work at a junkyard chop shop. They've got cutters, burners, crunchers," Boyking said.

"Too lightweight. You need heavy-duty hardware to crack that box," Viceroy said.

"Rob a construction site. There's all kinds of building going on at the approaches to Mountain," Cholla said.

Their big scheme was a long shot at best, but the chances for success dropped to zero a moment later when the Man came on the scene.

NINE

THE MAN SAID, "Git!"

Helmet-mounted extro-speakers broadcast the command loud enough for every Yahoo in the gap to hear it.

The stranger had entered the pass from the north, on foot, coming quite close to the scene before making his presence known. He stood on a rise ten feet above the base of the east cliff wall, about fifty feet away from the trapped prowler. He wore a bulky gray jumpsuit, gauntlets, battle boots, and a ring-collared helmet with the visor down. The visor was blanked, so that he could see out but nobody could see in.

He was big, and the oversized outfit he wore made him look bigger still. Fastened to his back like a knapsack was a boxy cerro-plastic container with rounded edges and a hooded top. A thick, flexible length of segmented armored tubing came out of the bottom of the box. Its other end was plugged into the butt of a hand-held device that looked something like a subgun. Thick, cumbersome, it measured three feet from muzzle to butt. The barrel took up a third of its length and had a nozzle-like tip. The stranger held it in his right hand, against his side, pointing downward.

The Yahoos were so flabbergasted by the intrusion that they didn't know how to react.

"Is that a *cop*?" Meneer said, amazed.

"Looks like," Cholla said.

It wasn't something they saw every day. Lawmen were even scarcer than honest citizens in Molehill.

"What's he doing here?"

"Becoming a statistic," Meneer said.

"How come the boys ain't ripping him up?"

"They probably think he's a hallucination."

"He's alone, too."

"He's got brass balls. Think I'll make me a pair of earrings out of them," Kharg said.

He was the one who had blasted the mek-arm earlier. He hefted his wheel auto-gun, bracing himself for the recoil.

"I always wanted to kill a cop," he said.

"Go easy on those bombshell rounds. We need them to bury the machine later."

"One's all it's gonna take, Meneer."

The other ninety-or-so Yahoos stood stupefied, not moving. Some were starting to growl and snarl and paw the earth, though.

The Man wanted to make sure his message got across.

"Get gone or get got," he said, sounding like he meant it.

The volatile Yahoos were quick to react to the threat, none quicker than the sniper.

A red dot glowed on the stranger's chest as the sniper lined him up in his laser-guided sights.

The stranger's auto-defense mechanisms struck first, quicker than thought. Sensors detected the laser light at first contact. A hatch no bigger than a matchbox cover popped open in the battle suit's padded right shoulder flange, the lid of a concealed mini-missile launcher.

A projectile the size of a toothpick streaked from the launcher tube, guided by a pinhead-sized micro-chip. A whiskery trail jetted from its tail as it raced to its goal, using the laser target-finder for its guide path.

The mini-missile rode the red ray back to its source and exploded on contact. The blast lit up the top of the west wall of the gap.

Rock chips and sniper shreds showered down like confetti.

Gunfire crackled on the gap floor as Yahoos shot at the stranger. Slugs sprayed in his direction, many scoring, knocking him back against the rock wall. More shooters were getting into his range with every passing second.

But the stranger stayed on his feet. His legs were bent and spread wide, his thick-booted feet were solidly planted. His back was braced against the cliff, and he leaned forward like a man fighting a stiff wind.

Scaled like a snake's skin, the charcoal-gray battle suit was made of wafered Fleximesh panels, a synthetic fabric that was one of the hardest and most durable substances on Earth. Heat- and cold-resistant, radiation-immune, antishock insulated, impervious to most acids and corrosive agents, the miracle fiber was malleable enough to be woven into battle suits, and lightweight enough to be worn without the aid of a hard robotized exo-skeleton. Fleximesh was also interwoven throughout the alternating laminated layers of metalloy and cerro-plastic that made up the helmet, to secure its structural integrity.

Sparks flashed where bullets struck the battle suit, so that the stranger seemed to be swarming with fireflies.

"What's keeping him up? Why don't he drop?"

Not only was the Fleximesh bulletproof, but its inter-molecular lattice weave blunted the impact of each hit by diffusing its kinetic energy throughout the battle suit. It protected like medium-grade hard armor at a fraction of the weight and discomfort and with far greater adaptability. As chain mail was to plate armor in the days of knighthood, so was Fleximesh to hard armor.

The barrage was noticeably weaker than earlier ones, much of the Yahoos' ammo having been used up in the fight with the prowler. Still, each hit felt like a punch or a kick to the Man, buffeting him on all sides. He stood it for the second or so that it took him to bring his weapon into play.

Liquid light, impossibly bright, speared a hundred feet from the nozzle, slicing straight through the middle of the massed Yahoos.

The weapon was a Holocauster plasmatic blowtorch, the twenty-first century's version of the old-fashioned flamethrower. But those earlier models had never thrown such a flame as this. Their fires were chemical; the Holocauster's was molecular. Originally designed as industrial equipment to work the ultra-tough composite alloys of the era, it had been conscripted as a weapon in the Last War.

The boxy container housed an energy excitation chamber where pressurized gases were bombarded by an electromagnetic flux so strong that they were transformed into a fourth state of matter: plasma. Not solid, liquid, or gas, but having characteristics of all three, the agitated plasma was a seething mass of man-made Hell on Earth.

Freed from the chamber that bred it, the plasma could not exist for more than a fractional millisecond. Superheated star stuff, it was not meant for this earth. When it broke down, it released energy in the form of heat.

And what heat! Sun fire, at a temperature of several thousand degrees Fahrenheit!

The nozzle gun was able to shoot the plasma thanks to a whirling magnetic funnel that projected from the muzzle when the trigger was pulled. The plasma remained plasma while it was in the intense magnetic field, which extended far enough away from the weapon and its wielder to protect them from the inferno when the plasma broke free of its magnetic matrix.

A hairline of liquid light leaped from the pinhole aperture in the muzzle. Beyond the magnetic vortex, it became a flaming sword a hundred feet long and a foot thick.

Splendid and terrible, it was blue at the edges, pearly pink in the middle, and white at the center. Snakes of light spiraled around the central shaft. Cataracts of noise poured from it as it superheated the surrounding air. Heat waves blurred the scene; light flashed to the summits of the gap's cliff walls.

The flaming sword vaporized all in its vicinity. A blowtorch would have had the same effect on a swarm of ants. It wasn't called the Holocauster for nothing. During the worst of the Last War, it had proved decisive in breaking the Chicom's human wave attacks.

The Man sprayed the plasmatic stream straight down the middle of the bunched Yahoos, swung it to the left, then to the right, then switched it off.

It was quick. The Yahoos were volatilized to their basic molecular makeup, vanishing into a puff of vapor one by one as they went under the giant plasmatic sword. Bodies disintegrated before the nerve cells could send the signals that mean pain.

Gale winds blew. The sky churned and boiled for a mile above the pass. Where the sword had passed, the ground melted and the rocks glowed red.

Winds rushed in from all directions. The Man lost his footing and sat down hard. Gusts tore at him. He braced himself with his back against the cliff.

Inside the battle suit it was a steam bath, despite the Fleximesh's marvelous insulating properties and a battery of mini-cooling units working on full capacity.

"Whew, that plasmatic sure packs a punch! Maybe too much!"

In-helmet mikes picked up his voice, amplifying it through speaker grids so he heard it at what seemed like normal volume. Without the audio boosters he wouldn't have heard it at all over the noise in the pass. He thought he sounded strained.

Molten ground congealed, hardening. Rocks lost their red color. Winds died down. The sky storm eased.

The Man was damned glad that he'd parked the cruiser in a safe place, hovering a half-mile up and well outside the danger zone of air turbulence caused by unleashing the plasmatic. He'd underestimated the power of the Holocauster. He'd brought the industrial cutting torch along to accomplish his main purpose, but the prospect of using it to eliminate the Yahoos had proved irresistible. A few minor adjustments to the stream flow check valve had disconnected the torch's built-in safety features, which were designed to prevent the tool from being used in just the way he had used it. A quick customizing job performed with the tip of his knife blade and a needle-fine burner ray had transformed the piece of construction equipment into a deadly anti-personnel device. It sure beat fighting a running gun battle against a hundred drug-crazed gangbangers, but the weapon was almost too much to handle, even for him. No worry that the cruiser had been too close to the affected area; its auto-defenses would have compelled it to evasive maneuvers to outrun the sky storm. And indeed, the steady signal readout from the airship proved that it was intact and unharmed.

Clouds crowded overhead, massing in columns that rose for miles. But the winds had died down on the ground.

The Man rose, scanning the scene. The quick-cooling ground had vitrified, becoming hard and glassy. A chemical analysis of the substance would reveal a high concentration of the trace elements that are the basic building blocks of the human body. That was all that remained of the Yahoos, who had become a permanent part of the landscape.

He made his way toward the prowler, the glassy ground crunching underfoot like crusty snow. The brittle shards would have cut ordinary footwear into ribbons within a few paces, but they were barely able to scuff his battle boots. Those boots had been built so tough that their wearer could step on a land mine and suffer nothing more than sore feet.

He'd been careful to keep the plasmatic stream well clear of the prowler. He'd spent a long time looking for it or its equivalents, and he wasn't going to risk damaging it just when his long search seemed to be close to an end.

The prowler was monitoring him. His detectors registered its spy rays. Through voice commands he keyed his transceiver to a tight beam frequency that was so old it was obsolete, long-forgotten by the world at large, though not by him or by those who had armed and armored him and sent him forth into the field to do battle.

The signal frequency was at the low end of the tight beam wave band and had been developed in the pioneering days of that communications mode. The signal-casting technique was clear and direct but required a great deal of power. A quarter-century of progress in the field had improved and refined the technology to new heights of superb efficiency, making the old system as outdated as the dinosaurs. But the old system had been new when it was first installed as the standard equipment of the APUs twenty years ago.

The communicator was heavy, bulky, and cumbersome because of the oversized power cells needed to supply the brute force to punch the signal through the ether. The Man had carried it with him for years without ever having the opportunity to use it for more than a routine commo check, to make sure it was still working.

He switched it on and signaled the prowler.

Readout displays shown on the inside of his visor told him that the signal was being transmitted. A pause followed, lasting only a few seconds in real time, but seeming to drag on and on, so great were the stakes for which he was playing.

Then:

"RECEIVING."

The prowler's reply came back to him on the same frequency. Taking a deep breath, the Man recited from memory a nine-digit series of numbers, the all-important universal recognition code that should override the APU's auto-defense mechanisms.

"INPUT RECEIVED."

Another pause, then:

"PROCESSING."

Delay now was dangerous, possibly fatal. Opposition far more formidable than the Yahoos was liable to come investigate the scene.

"RECOGNITION CODE ACCEPTED AND VALIDATED BY APU #805 SCOUT SERIES MODEL BIRD DOG. IDENTIFY, PLEASE."

"Smith, Texas Rangers," the Man said.

Sealed inside the locked box of the armored car was the key to a super-scientific technology that could alter the balance of power in Texas, the nation, and perhaps ultimately the world. For long weary years Smith had wandered alone in the wilderness seeking that key. Mastery of it meant that a long-delayed crusade for truth and justice could finally begin.

And yet, and yet . . . Smith's cause, the goal of his quest, was freedom. Freedom for those who deserved it and death for those who would destroy it. Such a goal could not be achieved by enslaving others who had earned the right to be free, not even when one of those others was a cybernetic construct such as Bird Dog.

APU recognition codes were the most jealously guarded secrets of the machines' makers, since they overrode the self-guided units' free will, subordinating them to the authority of the code-wielder. That secret, long lost to established officialdom, had been given to Ranger Command. With it, Smith could compel Bird Dog's obedience in almost all things, subject to certain restrictions. He could not order it to kill without justification. But as was seen in its dealings with the Yahoos, Bird Dog had a broad latitude of action where termination was involved.

It wasn't Bird Dog that Smith specifically required; any of the old APUs, with their cybernetic brains, would suit his special purpose. But only a handful of them were left, and they were scattered far and wide from the haunts of men. Smith would have to search long and hard to find another, if indeed any still remained to be found. Once or twice in the past he had been heartbreakingly close to his goal, only to have the unit in question destroyed before he got there.

To be cheated again on the verge of success would condemn him to an indeterminate stretch of lonely wanderings. But Smith played by his own rules, and they included giving Bird Dog the final say in its own fate. The prowler had labored for long years in its solitary mission to protect the public. Machines, too, can grow weary, and if Bird Dog craved the peace of nonexistence, it had earned it.

Smith offered it that choice.

"My instruments show that your body is damaged beyond repair but your brain is intact. I can take that brain and put it in another machine, if that's what you want."

"WHAT I WANT. . . ?"

"Or I can switch you off permanently. Downtime forever."

"END OF AWARENESS."

"Death, yes. So the choice is yours. Do you want to live or die?"

A long pause followed. Smith found himself checking his detectors for signs of incoming intruders. There were none so far, but each passing second increased the chances of being challenged.

Smith started to repeat his statement, but was interrupted in mid-sentence.

"THIS UNIT IS STILL COMPUTING THE COMBINATIONS OF YOUR PROPOSAL. QUESTION: WILL THE TRANSFER OPTION COMPROMISE MY MISSION TO PROTECT THE PUBLIC AND PRESERVE PRIVATE PROPERTY?"

"It will enable you to carry out your mission as never before. Use your Judge function, scan me to see if I speak the truth."

"THE JUDGE RULES THAT YOU SPEAK THE TRUTH—OR, RATHER, THAT YOU SPEAK WHAT YOU BELIEVE TO BE THE TRUTH."

"My mission is the same as yours."

"AGAIN, YOUR VERACITY IS CONFIRMED."

Warning buzzers sounded, alerting Smith to the approach of six aerial objects coming in from the south.

"Time's a-wasting. Delay too long means you choose death. So, what's it to be, life or death?"

"LIFE—"

"Good!"

"—IF YOU CALL THIS LIVING."

Was that supposed to be a joke? Smith had never heard of an APU with a sense of humor, but there had to be a first time for everything. He wasn't sure if it was a good sign or a bad sign, but finally he decided that a machine with a sense of humor was more human than a person without one.

Rima was a complicating factor. So were the six Maddog sky cycles flying in V-formation toward the pit and the pass.

The sky cycles were big two-man jobs with pilot and gunner riding back-to-back. Two pairs of side pods, mounted opposite each other at mid-fuselage, were armed with air-to-air and air-to-ground missiles—AAMs in the upper pods, AGMs in the lower pods. A firing stud in the handle of the pilot's control stick triggered a heavy machine gun underslung just aft of the nose, while his partner operated a lighter tail gun. The guns had computerized fire control; the missiles were guided by smart micro-chips. The aircraft flying lead in the V-wing also had a one-shot light beamer tube mounted topside on the nose.

This was the Maddogs' air force, one more reason why they were *the* gang to be reckoned with in Molehill. The gang leaders now knew that something had happened in the wasteland, but they didn't know what. They suspected it had something to do with "those asshole Yahoos," who had gone off their heads thanks to a shitload of Aggro. The drug was worth more than all the Yahoos put together and belonged to the Maddogs by right of might. The chiseling junior leaguers had been sentenced to lose their heads in punishment for their crime. The big blast that had lit up the night was more of a mystery. It looked like a bomb had gone off, but where would the Yahoos get that much explosive? Still, they had somehow managed to obtain the mega-dose of Aggro, so anything was possible.

The sky cycles went aloft to scout the scene. The crews were all stone sky bikers, skilled, reckless, fearless in the air, but even they had had to wait until the windstorm died down before daring to take off. Wiser heads would have delayed their flight even longer, but the Dogs' airmen had a reputation to maintain.

Winds beat at them, but they managed to keep some loose semblance of formation as they overflew the old highway and the pit. But when they neared the pass, a wicked updraft sent them hurtling hundreds of feet higher.

The seared landscape had cooled greatly, but the mean temperature at the floor of the pass was still 124 degrees Fahrenheit. That massive thermal tossed the sky cycles up into the clouds.

. And that bought Smith more time. He went to work on freeing the prowler.

He knew that the APU sheltered one "VIABLE FEMALE-TYPE LIFE FORM," as Bird Dog put it. His cruiser screens had depicted the prowler rescuing Rima as Smith raced to the scene. Had he known that she was an accomplice in several murders, his task would have been easier. Summary execution would have been her fate, for he could not leave her alive for the enemies who would come in his wake, infinitely dangerous foes who would pick her brain to glean every scrap of information about tonight's events. But Rima's crimes were unknown to him, and that made it necessary that he do his best to keep her alive.

She knew nothing of Smith, for the dialogue between him and Bird Dog had been conducted on the tight beam band. She knew that it had gotten intolerably hot in the compartment, though. She had sweated quarts and was near delirious from the suffocating blanket of heat.

There was a survival suit on board, but age and disuse had left it stiff, cracked, and inoperable.

Rima was shaken from unconsciousness by a violent pounding, a muffled hammering that vibrated through her bones.

Smith was digging out the prowler—a two-phase process, the first part of which required the use of the plasmatic blowtorch. The full-power blast of a few seconds' duration had depleted the gas tanks down to less than one-quarter full. Smith switched on the EMG flux in the chamber. It took a minute to reach full power. In the meantime, he unfastened the nozzle gun from its grooved recess holder in the back of the container and reset the choke valve, throttling it down until it was only a few notches above its lowest setting. That transformed it from a weapon of mass destruction back into a cutting tool again.

When the energy flux was powered up, a minute stream of gas molecules was fed into the chamber and excited into the plasma state.

Smith depressed the trigger, squirting a plasma burst at the biggest boulder in the rock pile pinning down the prowler. It was the size of a medium-class ground roadster, and others almost as large were lumped alongside it.

The nozzle spat a teardrop of plasma at the center of the boulder. It looked like a burning pearl, until it smashed on the rock, releasing all its energy. Light flashed; the rock reddened.

Smith did the same thing to the next largest boulder, and the next, and the next, until all of the big rocks had gotten the treatment. Alternating light and darkness created a strobing effect. Glaring flashes magnified Smith's shadow to gigantic proportions, while the darkness blotted it out an instant later.

After completing the process, he started the cycle again, beginning with the biggest boulder. The difference between the full-throttle plasma blast and these mini-bursts was the difference between a flood and a raindrop. Heating the rocks and allowing them to cool before heating them again created stresses that hastened their destruction.

A distant crash sounded a few miles to the west, as an out-of-control sky cycle hit the ground.

The others were still trying to fight their way down from the heights.

The turbulence was both a plus and a minus. Plus, because it kept the sky cycles away, at least temporarily. Minus, because it kept the cruiser from landing in the pass. The cruiser could hold a position high in the air without too much difficulty, but would be at great risk in the pass, where a sudden gust of hot wind could smash it against the cliffs. Without the cruiser, Smith was as good as dead. The turbulence, greatest near the ground, was lessening, but slowly, slowly.

The rocks were splintering and cracking from plasmatic heat stress. They became brittle. Some of the smaller ones exploded.

Smith put away the nozzle gun and drew his sidearm, backing away from the rocks. Mini-missiles were on hand if needed, but he thought explosive bullets could do the job now that the stones had been weakened. Best save the heavy artillery for targets that could shoot back.

Dropping into a crouch, he squeezed off short bursts from his machine pistol. Boulders fell apart from the explosive barrage, crumbling as if made of dust. Clouds of smoke and dirt rose from the mound, only to be beaten into shapelessness by the riotous winds.

Sky cycles flitted high overhead, spiraling downward toward the danger zone where they would present a real threat. The battle suit's heat suppressors shielded Smith's body from infrared imagers, but the pistol barrel and the Holocauster on his back would radiate definite heat signatures. The hot ground and cliffs would help to conceal them, however, and the hardware on the Maddog aircraft was probably none too sophisticated. Windblown murk would help hide Smith from visual sightings by the enemy crews.

He ordered the cruiser to begin its descent.

The cruiser was about a mile high, hovering with its underside parallel to the distant earth. Its nose dipped until it was pointing straight down at the ground. The auto-pilot switched off the tractor beam, that part of the great engine that drew a steady source of power from the Earth's magnetic field to keep the cruiser aloft. Deprived of that support, the cruiser dropped like a stone.

Winds screamed across the cruiser's surface in its mad dive. Its technology was so advanced that the limiting factor on its performance was its human pilot. It could bank and turn at such speeds that the multiple G forces would cause the pilot to black out. No human pilot was at the controls now, freeing the cruiser to operate at peak efficiency.

It didn't take long for the aircraft to fall most of a mile. As it neared a sky cycle, the tractors switched back on, drawing as much magnetic levitating force as needed to brake its hurtling dive. Its motive power was the planetary magnetic field, immense, awesome, inexhaustible. Jet engines were crude children's toys compared to magnetic levitation motors.

"Try to free yourself now," Smith said.

Much of the rock pile had been pulverized; much was still intact. Had enough of the crushing weight been removed for Bird Dog to power itself out?

The ground shook as the prowler fed power to the independent drive shafts of its buried wheels, sometimes separately, sometimes in combination. Not all the wheels were functioning.

The rock pile quivered, loose stones and dirt running down its sides like water. The rear of the vehicle shuddered. Rocks shifted and slid; dust showered into the air.

Bird Dog alternated power to the front and middle wheels, setting up a rocking motion. Another foot or so of the rear emerged into view, shaking so hard that it was a blur of motion. Shuddering from the effort, the machine poured on more power.

For an instant, Smith thought it was going to make the breakthrough—but no, it powered down, then idled, still caught in the mound's sucking grasp.

"UNABLE TO EFFECT RELEASE AT THIS TIME. ENGINE TEMPERATURE NEAR RED LINE. SUGGEST THAT YOU TRY AGAIN."

The lowest sky cycle had fought its way down to about a hundred feet above the top of the pass. Bobbing, it beat against the wind. The others were strung out above it in a loose, ragged spiral.

Bird Dog's labors had left it pouring out heat like a signal fire. The last thing Smith needed was for the airborne Dogs to drop a few rockets down his gullet.

He struck first. Not with the machine pistol, a close-quarters weapon; not with the four-barreled mini-missile launcher slung butt-first under his left arm; not with the beamer gun holstered on his left hip; and not with the plasmatic blowtorch.

With the cruiser.

The torpedo-shaped craft dropped into the scattered sky-cycle wing like a hawk among pigeons. Its speed had dropped to a hundred miles an hour or so, MagLev engines making a low moan.

When it was almost on top of the sky cycles, it opened fire. Its nose-mounted rotary cannon spewed big-caliber rounds in wholesale quantities. Hardened slugs clawed the two lowermost sky cycles. One exploded in midair. The other slanted sideways, smoke streaming from its engine. It slipped from view behind the pit's outside west wall, but could be heard blowing up an eye blink later.

Nose lifting, the cruiser started to pull out of its dive, but not before grazing one of the three remaining sky cycles. The edge of a stubby mid-body stabilizing fin brushed the rim of a grilled rotor canopy in passing. Just a nudge, like a motorcycle being nudged by an express train. It doesn't do much to the train, but it sure plays hell with the motorcycle. So, too, the sky cycle, which, similarly nudged, was flung tumbling across the sky and sent crashing into the flats north of the pass.

A fourth sky cycle hung well outside the cone-shaped field of the nose cannon's fire. The crew thought that they had escaped immediate death when the cruiser's bow gun dipped below them. They hadn't. A side gun spat at them, far lighter than the rotary gun, but still lethal.

Smith flattened as the riddled wreck came hurtling down toward him and crashed in the pass. He kept his head down. Seconds later, the super-heated hydrogen fuel exploded. The aircraft had a relatively small fuel tank and had expended much of its store fighting the windstorm. Even so, it was still quite a respectable blast. Red-hot shrapnel whizzed through the air as following a fragmentation bomb. Shards scored the cliffs above Smith's head, but he was unhit.

The fifth and last sky cycle was caught in the downdraft as the cruiser plummeted past it. It was sucked groundward for fifty yards before tearing free of the vacuum stream.

Its flight path sharply curving, the cruiser pulled out of its dive and leveled off, flashing south toward Molehill.

The sky cycle fired both AAMs, then banked sharply, beginning a series of evasive maneuvers.

Twin fire-tailed rockets arrowed toward the cruiser, closing from above and to the rear, fast narrowing the gap.

The cruiser fired thermal flares to the right and peeled off to the left, climbing steeply.

Firing from a prone position, Smith loosed all four barrels of his mini-missile launcher at the sky cycle. He feared that it would fire its AGMs at the prowler on general principle.

There was a chance that his action would attract the sky cycle's notice and provoke it to do the very thing that he feared, but he was willing to take that chance. He preferred action to inaction, especially in a shooting scrape.

He didn't wait for the result; he scrambled to put some space between himself and the place from which he had fired. The prop wash from the sky cycle's rotors fanned the air, its motor puttering noisily over the pass.

It was a chancy shot, even with all four mini-missiles engaged. The sky cycle was about a hundred yards distant; the mini-missile's range maxed out at five hundred feet, but that was under optimum launching conditions, in clear still air. Gusty thermals rising up from the pass would not improve the accuracy of the heat-seeking minis.

As it turned out, only one of them got through to hit the target, but one was enough. It didn't take much to knock down a sky cycle. A crump sounded in midair, like a baseball bat knocking a ball into the stands for a home run. That was the sound of the mini-missile impacting the motor housing, where the aircraft's heat signature was strongest.

The sky cycle lurched. Shrapnel tore through the mesh grille, into the rotors, smashing the blades out of shape. The aircraft heeled over. It got off one AGM but fired it straight into the sky because it was upside down.

The AGM rocketed upward in a parabolic arc, peaked, and arched downward, exploding somewhere in the wastes far to the east.

The sky cycle hit the cliff backward and upside-down, bounced off the east wall, and crashed outside the pass near the west wall, burning furiously.

At the same time, the cruiser was fleeing the paired AAMs.

The AAM nearest the thermal flare curved after it, caught it, and detonated on contact.

The other wavered a bit uncertainly toward the flare, then chose to ignore it, continuing its pursuit of the cruiser. It lacked the maneuverability of the MagLev machine, which now zoomed upward at a fantastic rate.

Trying to pull out of its dive, the AAM nosed up just in time to avoid hitting the rubble wall of the old highway. It skimmed over the top in a low arc that took it straight into the skyline of Glitter Gulch.

The blast took a bite out of the strip's gaudy neon rainbow.

Smith's voice command directed the cruiser to reverse course. Curving up and away from Molehill, it made a wide 180-degree turn and flew north. It flew upside-down with as much facility as if it were right-side-up, especially when there was no human pilot aboard to protest.

Smith resumed work on freeing the prowler. He hoped explosive bullets would do the trick. He didn't relish advertising his presence with the incandescent plasmatic torch now that the attention of all Molehill was riveted north of the old highway. Not to mention the Citadel in Mountain, with its impressive array of high-tech scanners and detectors. The explosive bullets weren't exactly discreet, either.

Bird Dog's rear wheels were undamaged and now well-greased thanks to the lube job provided by the Yahoos who had gone under them. If they could only get some traction . . .

Big rocks wedged beneath the prowler raised its rear wheels off the ground. Get rid of the rocks, bring the back wheels into play, and it just might be enough to free the vehicle.

Selecting single-fire mode on his machine pistol, Smith fired into the rock heap under Bird Dog, placing his shot with precision. When he saw that it was not enough, he fired again.

The vehicle dipped, dropping its rear by a good two feet. Not good enough.

Smith put a few more in. It was like excavating with a slow-motion jackhammer. Not so slow—the prowler was moving again.

When it stopped its descent, the rear wheels were only a few inches above the ground. The prowler settled another inch, snuggling in, but no more than that.

Smith couldn't stand to be bilked so close to success. He climbed on top of the vehicle, walked to the end, and stood toeing the rear edge, adding his 225 pounds and another 50 pounds of hardware to the total weight pressing the rock pile. He flexed his knees, pushing downward to give a little extra oomph.

That did it. The rear wheels grounded, leveled, then sank another six inches as the weight shifted some more. Now the vehicle was tilted slightly downward.

Smith climbed down fast and stepped aside while Bird Dog did its thing. The rear wheels turned, digging in, whipping up dirt and stones in great brown spouts. They grooved deep into the earth.

The prowler didn't break free on its first attempt, or even its fourth. But with the help of the rear wheels, alternating with the other sets, it worked up a good, strong rocking motion—reversing, fighting for every inch, gaining as much ground as possible, then suddenly going forward, slamming deeper into what remained of the rock pile, tearing loose, then reversing to start another cycle.

The cruiser flashed over the pass, dropped behind the far side of the cliffs, and settled to a landing on the flats north of the pit's east wall.

A surface-to-air missile arced after it in pursuit, fired from somewhere in the Gulch. The SAM was tiny, probably from a shoulder-mounted launcher. It angled upward over the cliffs, but its crude sensors lost the cruiser nestled in the lee at the foot of the rocks on the other side.

It fizzled out somewhere to the north.

Bird Dog crashed out. Dirt and rocks sprayed everywhere as it tore free of its premature burial mound. Loosed all at once from the rock pile's paralyzing grip, the vehicle lunged backward at high speed from an excess of power. Heaps of debris slid off its top and sides as it slewed around in a tight curve and stopped.

The mek-arm was broken. The turret was crushed, barring use of the rotary gun. Only two of the wheels on the port side worked. Most of the armor forward of the turret was pretty badly banged up. The glacis plate, the strongest and thickest piece of shielding on the prowler, was intact, but badly scuffed and knocked out of joint, with the thinner plates butted up against it. The vehicle wobbled; some wheels were out of alignment.

But its cybernetic brain was secure and unharmed, and that's all that mattered. Plus, it was still mobile.

Smith mounted the prowler, sitting with his back against the front of the turret and his legs sticking out in front of him. He switched on the battle suit's mag clamps, glueing himself to the vehicle, whose composite armor plates contained enough magnetizable metalloy to bind the attraction.

"Let's get out of here!"

"READING YOU LOUD AND CLEAR, RANGER SMITH."

The prowler was already in motion, jostling into the pass, heading north. It was a rough ride for Smith, a bone-jarring bucking bronco. The mag clamps kept him from being thrown, but did nothing to soften the jolts of a bumpy forty-five-MPH run across rough terrain.

It got rougher when the Maddogs started shooting at them from the top of the old highway. Small-arms fire, mostly, from a relative handful of shooters. The gang had some Ninja Jeeps, fast attack vehicles that were basically customized dune buggies armed with heavy machine guns, recoilless rifles, rocket launchers, and other hard-hitting weapons of destruction. But the FAVs couldn't climb the steep rubble walls of the collapsed roadway. They had a long way to go before they could bring their guns to bear on Smith and the prowler, detouring east along the rampart for several miles, to a pass that would spill them down to the lowlands outside the cratered walls of the pit. There was nothing for the Maddogs to do but take the route as fast as possible and hope to intercept the fugitives in time.

Truckloads of Dogs rolled up to the rubble walls. The gangbangers clambered to the top and started shooting at the prowler. More were arriving every minute, now that the gang had mobilized into action. Scattered firing ripened into a barrage of many guns, so that the scene sounded like a shooting range.

The pass became a gauntlet of gunfire. Many slugs spanged off the prowler's rear. Its wobbling, erratic gait kept it from being hit more often. Smith held his head down, glad for the turret's bulk between him and the bullets.

Some small fires still burned where a sky cycle had crashed near the midpoint of the gap's west wall. The wreck north of that wall blazed brighter still. The prowler passed the first and neared the second as the gunfire steadily increased.

An explosive bullet or mini-missile tagged Bird Dog. Mini-missile, probably—it was a hard hit. Smith would have been thrown from his perch if not for the mag clamps. Fleximesh armor neutralized the blow, but still he suffered a pretty bad bruising.

Rock walls rolled away on both sides, and then Bird Dog broke into the open, clear of the gap.

The north flats were vast, rugged plains stretching to the horizon and beyond. No standing structures and very few ruins interrupted the landscape. Some low hills dotted the prairie, so distant that they looked like gopher mounds.

Dark, rushing clouds lowered the ceiling of the big sky to a few hundred feet above the ground. Firelight from the burning wreck fought a losing battle against night's blackness.

West, a crystal spear blade poked at the bottom of the clouds. It was the topmost tower of the Citadel in Mountain, Boss Claggard's stronghold. Mists and murk hid the rest of the walled city.

What did Claggard and his security chief, ruthless, efficient Burton Floyd, make of the mayhem in Molehill? So far the boss had stayed out of it, holding his forces in check.

May he continue to do so, thought Smith. Mountain was a rich fortress city-state, with the latest in high-tech armaments and a skilled, disciplined private army. Floyd was a master of secret police skullduggery and covert operations, a prize asset of his tough, ambitious boss.

Dangerous men, both of them, though not nearly as dangerous as they'd have been if they could have seen Smith and the cruiser as they really were. But the cruiser's signal-suppressing silent-running cloak screened it to near invisibility, negating most detectors, scanners, spy-rays, and beam probes. The battle suit was cloaked, too. It was impossible to hide something like the plasmatic blowtorch, so Smith had worn a partial cloak. Full cloak would have made it appear on the detector screens that an invisible man was wielding the Holocauster. That would surely have stung Claggard and Floyd into action!

Instead, he'd adjusted the cloak to counterfeit the EMG wave patterns typical of an adventurer or soldier of fortune suited up in ordinary light body armor with minimal cybernetic abilities. A false EMG trail to throw off the trackers.

Bird Dog rounded the curve of the east outer wall, beyond the line of fire. It was darker and quieter. Thorn bushes and patches of prickly pear cactus were scattered over pocked fields.

The big black wall of the cliffs rose up and up. The cruiser sat in a cove at its base, about a quarter-mile east of the pass. Bird Dog made for it.

A snake of motion slithered into view as it rounded the far curve of the east wall, about a mile away. A column of Ninja Jeeps, racing to intercept the fugitives.

The prowler slammed to a stop near the cruiser.

"You know what has to be done now," Smith said.

"PROCEED, RANGER."

Smith declamped, freeing himself to move. The forward top hatch was too damaged to unseal itself and open. Explosive bolts fired, blowing the hatch off its hinges. The compartment below served a dual function as bomb disposal carrier and people carrier. It was one of the best-protected areas of the vehicle.

Inside, a figure lay curled on its side in the knee-chest position, shrouded in dripping sudsy folds of pneumatic cushioning, completely enveloped.

Rima.

The air bag had cocooned her, its permeable membranes having sprayed her with protective chemical foam earlier to insulate her from the intense heat of the Holocauster. The foam was impregnated with oxygen so she could breathe.

She wasn't moving. Heat waves wafted out of the hatchway. The air bag was limp and steaming, like an overcooked leafy vegetable.

Smith pulled Rima out and carried her in his arms to the cruiser. Tossing her over his shoulder would have been easier, but the air bag was in the way.

The clear bubble canopy opened; the boarding ladder unfolded. Smith eased Rima's inert form to the ground. Grabbing a double fistful of the air bag's folds, he tore it open, uncovering its occupant.

Rima lay on her back, eyes closed, not moving. A glow from the cruiser's instrument panel fell on her face. Cosmetic dyes had washed off and her skin shone with chemical oils. Even without makeup she had black brows and thick lashes and a spoiled, wicked red mouth. Strands of bubbly white foam clung to her.

She was alive, breathing. Smith peeled her out of the bag, draining a mass of glycerine-like insulating fluids from its shredded membranes. They puddled on the ground, not soaking in.

She stirred when he picked her up again. Her head turned to the side, foamy fluid draining from her nose and mouth. She choked, gasped, coughed, spewed out a pint more fluid—all without regaining consciousness.

Smith carried her up the ladder and lowered her into the padded seat behind the pilot's. Safety harnesses slipped into position, securing her.

Smith switched on the inboard robo-doc. Bulbs lit, relays closed, and the auto-medic went to work tending the patient. Smith caught a quick glimpse of Rima's face just before a descending oxy-mask covered it below the eyes. She was young, vital, feral, beautiful.

She'd be surprised when she awakened . . .

He'd have saved Bird Dog first and then done what he could for the girl later, but the prowler didn't want it that way. It was mission-oriented. Protecting Rima was its mission and it was determined to see it through. Stowing her safely on the cruiser was quicker than arguing the matter with the APU, Smith reasoned.

The cruiser was going to be unsafe indeed, if the Ninja Jeeps got much closer. The aircraft's cloak confused their sensors with its misleading signals, but when the FAV crews made a visual sighting of it and the prowler, they would cut loose with everything they had.

Bird Dog opened a hatch in its port side. Smith knelt beside the opening and stuck his upper body inside it. His shoulders were just barely able to fit.

A hidden panel opened in a bulkhead to his right, baring a rectangular recess the size of a brick. Within lay a series of red and black switches. Smith flipped the red switches up and the black switches down.

A click sounded. A small square lid rolled up in the space between the top and bottom rows of switches. Inside a shallow niche were two keyholes, side by side. Inside the keyholes were two keys, protruding from the holes.

Smith turned both keys toward each other until he heard a bolt thunk into place.

The seemingly solid bulkhead opposite the hatchway slid back, exposing a dull gray-green oblong panel. A handgrip in its center was surrounded by a number of jacks and sockets.

Smith took hold of the handgrip and pulled. A long, heavy box emerged, so heavy that he needed both hands to hold it. Removing it from its compartment, he set it down on the ground near the armored car.

Similar in size and shape to a ten-gallon jerrican, its gray-green composite cabinet was studded with more jacks and plugs. It weighed about seventy-five pounds. It vibrated constantly from ceaseless internal processes.

It was Bird Dog.

The cabinet housed the APU's cybernetic brain, which was where the self-aware entity named Bird Dog resided.

This was the core unit, the basic component, the software that made it a prowler. All the rest of the armored car was just machinery.

In addition to the cylindrical liquid crystal core that was the brain, the box was crammed with stacked micro-circuitry blocks, photonic synapse transfers, pyramidal threshold gates, buffers, amplifiers, a mile's worth of hard-wired fiber optics, and other cybernetic adjuncts that made up the thinking machine's nervous system. A self-contained battery of rechargeable energy cells supplied the power. Sensors monitored the outside world, transceivers provided the comm links, and an auto-defense system served as the prowler's shield and sword.

Smith picked up the box by the handle and carried it to the cruiser's cargo hold amidships. He stowed it away, securing it for the flight.

"All set?"

"READY FOR TAKE-OFF, RANGER."

"Glad to have you aboard."

The cargo hatch sealed shut. A final task remained. Smith unfastened the Holocauster harness and shrugged out of the rig. He loaded it in the armored car's portside compartment, placing the nozzle gun in the niche previously filled by the cybernetic brain. He switched the controls from manual to remote. The tool was often used in hazardous environments hostile to human life, requiring the operator to manipulate it by remote control.

Smith jogged back to the cruiser, climbing into the cock-pit. Safety harnesses automatically strapped him in, the canopy closed, and the ladder retracted.

Smith hit the altitude control. The invisible tractor-beam cone battened on the earth's magnetic lines of force, tapping into them to power the cruiser's superconductive MagLev engines.

The cruiser shot straight up into the sky, sucking up a spout of dirt in its wake.

Sullen storm clouds crackled, heavy with charge. Crook-ed lightning jumped from cloud to cloud as the cruiser neared the underside of the low storm ceiling.

Smith triggered the red firing button of his hand-held remote unit. Far below, the Holocauster responded by unleashing an annihilating plasmatic burst inside the hulk of the armored car.

Sun fire flashed at ground zero, lighting up the night. The explosion of the vehicle's hydrogen fuel tanks and ammunition stores was consumed in the infinitely greater inferno of the plasmatic blowtorch eating itself.

A pillar of fire thrust two hundred feet into the air, spun, wavered, then collapsed.

The Ninja Jeep column halted. Some of the FAVs whose broadsides faced the blast were turned over by the concussion.

When the shock waves passed, Maddog gunners peppered the sizzling blast site with rockets, artillery shells, and heavy machine-gun fire. The barrage did little more than blister the landscape and let the Dogs blow off some steam.

Lightning bolts cracked the sky, accompanied by booming peals of thunder. The electrical storm spooked a trigger-happy gunner into firing blindly into the clouds. The shots came nowhere near the cruiser, which was out of sight, but at least the Dog was in the right ballpark.

The clouds tore open, drenching the Maddogs in a furious downpour.

Thunder and lightning were as harmless as rain to the cruiser, which was well-grounded and insulated against massive electrical shocks. Hull-mounted accumulator intake nodes could transform the energy from direct hits by lightning bolts into storable power for the battery cells. Its makers had built the cruiser to survive a variety of storms, both natural and manmade.

The torpedo-shaped aircraft climbed above the clouds, into the starry heights where the night air was thin, clear, and calm. Soaring high above the storm, it set a new course and went on its way.

Destination: showdown.

TEN

"ANYBODY FINDS US, I'll have to blip them, Mr. Guthrie."

"That's why I pay you, Breedlove. To kill people."

"Yes, sir, and quite handsomely, too."

"So what are you bellyaching for?"

"You misread me, sir. I made no complaint. As you may have observed, I enjoy my work."

"Maybe too much."

"Call it pride of professionalism. No *pistolero* was ever much good without it. But I do like to kill people, yes sir, very much so. But not when it might run me afoul of Commissioner Piper."

Dan Guthrie stood up, knocking over his folding chair. He had to be careful not to hit his head on the low ceiling of the prefab mini-dome that served as the command post for this secret base northwest of Mountain.

Resting his big fists on top of the suspensor panel that was the commanding officer's desk, he leaned forward until his face was only a few inches from Breedlove's.

"If you've got something to say, spit it out, mister!"

"You're way off your turf, sir. An encounter with some of Boss Claggard's Mountain Men could have serious repercussions for the Commissioner. If your presence here becomes known, it could be a *casus belli*—"

"A *what*?"

"Cause for war, sir."

"Why didn't you say that in the first place? Never mind. Don't leave any witnesses and Claggard won't have a case."

"I never do. Leave witnesses. Sir. But premature exposure might jeopardize the timetable for conquest."

"For a blipster you sure talk like a damned politician, Breedlove."

"Begging your pardon, sir. It's just that I wouldn't want to be held to account for upsetting Mr. Piper's plans without a very good reason. That's even more hazardous duty than I would care to undertake."

"If that's what's griping you, relax. I'll take full responsibility for whatever happens, so you don't have to worry about covering your ass with the commissioner. Satisfied?"

"Yes, sir."

"I suppose you'd like me to put it in writing?"

"No, sir, your oral statement is good enough for me."

"It is, huh? Well, that's awfully good of you, old top. Now get your ass out of here and go and do your goddam job."

"Sir," Breedlove said.

He turned and stepped to the mini-dome's entrance flap. He paused to unseal it.

"And tell Gottschalk to get his ass in here. After all, it is his office," Guthrie said, chuckling.

Hot white sunlight burst through the open entryway as Breedlove went outside. The intense light bleached the details out of his figure, making it a silhouette outlined by the portal.

He resealed the flap, muting the terrible light.

Outside, there was no relief. The mini-coolers in Breedlove's broad-brimmed hat and loose garments labored to beat the heat down to tolerable levels. Wraparound UV-blocking sunshades filtered out the blinding glare so he could see clearly.

The secret base was hidden in a pocket canyon opening off a dry wash in an arid, near-desert landscape. It wasn't in the Badlands but was close enough to them to be virtually uninhabitable. The site was well off the land and aerial trade routes and even the smugglers' trails. Desolation made for a good hiding place.

It was a small facility, as it had to be to be planted under the very noses of Boss Claggard and his security chief. The biggest thing in it was the Raptor V/STOL plane, which was parked on a makeshift landing pad at the far end of the canyon. Chameleon camouflage tarps covered it, mimicking the gray, tan, and brown color scheme of the surroundings and cloaking the vehicle from signal detection. The pilot sheltered in a one-man tent dome pitched under the plane, ready to scramble at first alert.

The advance base was now primarily an observation post. Later, as the pace of covert ops against Mountain was stepped up, it would serve as a supply dump and ultimately a staging area for some of the invasion force. But that day was still in the future, and for now it was a minimal, low-profile installation.

A few mini-domes nestled in a shady cleft under a rocky overhang on the canyon wall. They were cloaked and camouflaged. One was the CO's office, doubling as his quarters. A second housed the five-man permanent party. A third held water and food rations and other supplies. A fourth was the comm shack, with its communicators, computers, and monitoring devices. A fifth was the armory. Latrines were dug far away from the encampment. The motor pool was located in a side pocket on the opposite side of the canyon. Vehicles included a wheeled armored personnel carrier with hovercraft capability, two wide-wheeled all-terrain one-man scout vehicles, a two-man combat sky cycle, five one-man sky cycles, and a couple of hover-bikes, one-man hovercraft that rode on a column of compressed air. All were camoed and cloaked.

Captain Dieter Gottschalk was base commander. He was a professional soldier, an officer and a mercenary. He was working for Guthrie and didn't squawk when Guthrie commandeered his mini-dome for the duration of his visit. Breedlove found him in the comm shack.

"Your college boy said that you wanted to see me," Gottschalk said.

He stood under the dome, facing Guthrie, who was sitting behind his desk.

"Breedlove? He's a snotty punk, all right," Guthrie said.

"Why don't you get rid of him?"

"He can shoot. Besides, he's a spy for the commissioner. Thinks I don't know that he's been telling tales about me to Piper."

"Why tell me?"

"Hell, Dieter, I figured you already knew."

Gottschalk neither confirmed nor denied the statement. "All the more reason to get rid of him."

"Why? With him gone, Piper might put in another spy that I don't know. This way, he's happy and I'm happy."

"As you wish," Gottschalk said, shrugging. "Still, the desert is large enough to hide one more body."

"That an offer?"

"Merely an observation. Of course, if the price is right . . ."

"Forget it. That's not what I called you in to talk about. Besides, Breedlove's not so easy to take as he looks. He's fast."

Gottschalk smiled. His white, even teeth contrasted with skin tanned and cracked like old leather. His hair was so blond it was almost white. He had pale eyebrows, so fine and thin that they seemed virtually nonexistent, and gray eyes.

"Sit down and make yourself comfortable," Guthrie said.

"You are too kind."

"Hell, it's your office."

There were two chairs in the space, each an ultra-light tubular piece that could be folded up to the size of a thermos bottle. Guthrie sat in one of them. Gottschalk took the other.

"I'm the guy who kicks the butts, Dieter. That's why they pay me. So whose butt do I kick for the mess at Salt Lick?"

"The officer in charge is responsible for everyone under his command."

"I wouldn't even try to kick your butt. With those fancy martial arts tricks of yours, I'd wind up with my foot up my ass."

Gottschalk smiled with his lips, keeping his teeth covered.

"But give me something that I can give Piper to keep him off my back," Guthrie said.

"Hazards of war, pure and simple, that's the reason. I sent a three-man squad to set up an electronic warfare nest in Salt Lick to disrupt Mountain's communications and signal intelligence for when the campaign moves into its active phase. It was all done according to plan, part of the timetable. Salt Lick is a prime location for EW ops. It's isolated, uninhabited, and in a position to intercept the bulk of the Citadel's signal traffic. The squad's mission was to prepare the nest for future ops. By sheer bad luck, they were discovered by an enemy patrol making a routine sweep across the area. Just one of those random unpredictabilities of life.

"In the firefight that followed, the patrol was destroyed— by conventional weapons, guns, not E-weps. One of the squad was killed: Teazle, an EW tek, a civilian contract agent on leave from his job at Powergrid in Santone. The others were unable to recover the body before enemy reinforcements arrived. Rather than leave it behind, they destroyed it with a class 2 burner, then escaped."

"Things would have been a whole lot simpler for everybody if they hadn't used an illegal E-wep," Guthrie said.

"That was the only way that the body could be completely destroyed, obliterated without a trace. Otherwise there would have been enough left of the remains for investigators to type for DNA patterns—hard evidence which could have been linked to Santone, since all Powergrid employees' genetic fingerprints are on file."

"Sounds logical to me."

"And to me. I would have done the same thing in their place. Besides, Hostiles have been known to have class 2 weps and above. Everything else about the incident points to a roving band of Hostiles as the culprits."

Guthrie sat back. "We can improve on that."

"How?"

"Give Floyd some real Hostiles. Rig things so the searchers think they've found the guilty parties. They'll be dead, but the finders won't know that. It'll look like they were killed in a firefight after they were discovered. We'll fix that up, too. Plant a remote launcher, have it fire on a patrol so the attack points to the Hostiles. Floyd's men will do the rest. They'll find a class 2 burner in the camp, the one used on Teazle—you have it, don't you?"

"Yes."

"That'll tie it all up in one neat package."

"Where will you get the Hostiles?"

"There's always plenty of them around, even in this godforsaken hell. You just have to know where to look for them. And if there're none to be found, we'll just have to dress up some volunteers as Hostiles and kill them. Always plenty of volunteers in Piper's political prisons."

Gottschalk considered the matter for a moment. "It could work. That Floyd's a sharp one, though."

"Finding the class 2 wep with the dead men should clinch it. Besides, he'll have bigger things to worry about pretty soon."

"Do you want me to handle the, uh, arrangements?"

"No. Piper's got experts at faking evidence. They'll handle it. I don't want any attention drawn to this area, either. Claggard's got the wind up over the lost patrol and the action in Molehill last night. Stay low and let things cool down for a while before you resume ops. As cool as they're ever going to get in a place where the temperature at high noon reaches 125 degrees," Guthrie said.

"All bets are off if Floyd found that EW nest, though. In that case, we're totally screwed," he added.

"The nest is secure, as I believe I said earlier, a number of times."

"I like to hear you say it again."

"The nest is underground and is shielded by a passive cloaking device. It only works when a spy ray or beam probe impacts it, and then only emits signals that duplicate those of its surroundings."

"How do you know that Floyd hasn't already found it?"

"Any contact with detector energies would trigger a tight-beam alarm signal to our receiver here, and that hasn't happened. Also, physical tampering with the nest will cause it to self-destruct."

"Maybe Floyd's staking it out to see who comes to it."

"Then he'll have a long wait. Once the hardware is installed, the nest is operated by remote from here. But I'm an action ops man, not counterintelligence. If you're that worried about it, I'll order it to self-destruct."

"No, don't do that. Unless you feel it's necessary. Use your own discretion."

"Tossing the ball back in my court, eh, Mr. Guthrie?"

"As field commander, you're closer to the situation than anyone else."

"Thank you. I feel that leaving the nest in place is an acceptable risk at this time. It's already been paid for with the life of one of my men. I'd hate to throw it away without a good reason to do so."

"It's your call. And your neck," Guthrie said.

Gottschalk nodded.

Guthrie leaned forward. "You say that the nest has a passive cloak."

"Yes."

"Pretty advanced stuff."

"State of the art, I believe."

"No wonder the prowler didn't stumble across the nest. They didn't have passive cloaks back when it was built."

"I didn't know that there were any of them left."

"There's one less after last night. But there's still a few of them out there in the boondocks. This one was a scout, basically designed to sniff out illegal E-weps. It must have registered the discharge fired at Salt Lick and come looking for the burner. A class 2 wep would have a high priority for it. It tracked it as far as Molehill before losing the trail. Somehow it got in a fracas with the locals and messed them up pretty good before being destroyed."

"How does that affect the campaign?"

"I don't know. I'll know better when the data I'm waiting for comes in," Guthrie said.

Ten minutes later, Breedlove entered the dome.

"It's customary to request permission to enter the CO's office," Gottschalk said.

"You'll have to forgive me, Captain. I'm a civilian," Breedlove said.

"Yes," Gottschalk said, scowling.

"From home base?" Guthrie said.

"From Mountain, sir. The Citadel."

"Give it here."

Breedlove handed Guthrie a sealed black message capsule. He said, "I just happened to be in the comm shack when it came in, so I volunteered to deliver it to you. Anything to help out our brave boys in uniform, you know."

"Bah!" Gottschalk's face showed open contempt.

"I know you're a busy man, Captain, so I won't keep you from your other duties," Guthrie said.

Gottschalk took the hint and exited.

"I afraid the captain is none too fond of me," Breedlove said.

"Hell, I don't much like you myself."

"No, but I'm useful to you, Mr. Guthrie. That's even better. Sir."

Guthrie laid the message capsule on the desktop. He input a five-digit transcription code number on a keypad inset in his wrist guard and pressed the transmit button. An answering beep from the capsule signaled that the transmission had been accepted and input. Inside the capsule was a coded message in the form it had been received at the comm shack. The message was gibberish without the transcription code. The correct code number was input to the capsule's micro-computer, which then used that code to decipher the message. A mini-laser printer scanned a roll of photosensitive plasti-paper inside the capsule, putting the translated message into hard copy.

The comm shack's transceivers had a copy of the raw message, but without the code key a battery of super-computers working nonstop couldn't decrypt it in a thousand years.

Three short beeps from the capsule announced that the process was finished.

Guthrie's personal detectors registered no traces of electronic surveillance. Pausing with his hand on the capsule, he nodded toward the entrance.

Breedlove catfooted to the door and unsealed the flap to find Gottschalk just outside, eavesdropping.

"Yes, Captain?"

"Bah!"

Turning on his heel, Gottschalk stalked away, ramrod-straight under the brutal sun. Breedlove watched him until he disappeared inside the comm shack.

He resealed the flap. "All clear, sir."

Guthrie unscrewed the capsule into two halves, removing a tightly rolled sheet of plasti-paper that was four inches long and a half-inch wide. Putting the capsule halves an arm's length away from him on the desk, he unrolled the communiqué.

The capsule halves melted into black puddles. They turned into thin wisps of purple smoke, curling against the domed ceiling.

Guthrie held the missive with both hands to keep it from scrolling as he read it.

It was from one of Piper's spies, a highly placed turncoat on Claggard's staff.

It read:

"RESPONDING TO YOUR PREVIOUS INQUIRY. THE FOLLOWING HAS BEEN DETERMINED:

"1. NO UNIDENTIFIED AIRCRAFT WERE TRACKED BY CITADEL DETECTORS DURING MOLEHILL OUTBREAK LAST NIGHT. MONITORS DID REGISTER SIGNAL ANOMALIES IN AREA DURING THE TIME IN QUESTION, BUT

THESE WERE ASCRIBED TO INSTRUMENT ERROR BY OPERATORS ON DUTY. NUMEROUS EYEWITNESS ACCOUNTS REPORT SIGHTING AIRCRAFT OF UNKNOWN ORIGIN, POSSIBLY MAGLEV-TYPE CRUISER.

"2. INVESTIGATION REVEALS THAT APU WAS NOT DESTROYED BY ROCKETS AND ARTILLERY, AS PREVIOUSLY BELIEVED, BUT RATHER WAS INCINERATED BY HEAVY-DUTY PLASMATIC TORCH.

"3. CHEMICAL ANALYSIS OF APU'S REMAINS FINDS NO TRACE OF COMPOUND ELEMENTS ASSOCIATED WITH LIQUID CRYSTAL COLLOID MATERIAL OR CONTAINER FOR SAME. THIS INDICATES THAT CYBERNETIC BRAIN WAS REMOVED FROM APU PRIOR TO ITS DESTRUCTION.

"—MESSAGE ENDS—"

Guthrie slammed a fist against the desk, hammering it down by eighteen inches before the suspensors arrested its descent and buoyed it up.

"It's *him*, by God! It can't be, but it is! Hell and damnation!"

"Him who, Mr. Guthrie?"

"Smith! *Smith!*"

ELEVEN

GUTHRIE HAD LAST seen Smith five years earlier, when they were flying a suicide run against Juggernaut at the Battle of the Capitol Steps during Austin's Violent Night in A.D. 2030.

It was a time of troubles, as always. The fedgov, headquartered in New Washington, Maryland, had gone broke again. The day the checks bounced, rioting erupted in twenty-five major Old Cities where the urban underclass was concentrated. Nine regional power centers claimed to be the seat of the legitimate national government of the United States, but none of them offered to pick up the tab. On the heels of the recent mega-quake that had submerged much of the Pacific Coast (the old one; there was a new and different shoreline since the quake), it seemed that the Four Horsemen of the Apocalypse were saddling up for a good long ride.

Texas was swarming with hordes of hundreds of thousands of dispossessed men, women, and children. A vengeful Nature had left them homeless in the wake of the great eco-catastrophes. Refugees fled the drowned cities of the Gulf Coast, the broken lands of the Balcones Fault, the infernal fire and ash of the volcanic Vulcan Belt, and the cyclonic storms of Tornedo Alley in the Panhandle. Bandits, famine, and plague were everywhere.

Have-nots wandered the land in great migratory bands, seeking shelter that was nowhere to be found. Masses of them were encamped outside every city in the state. Used to doing for itself with a minimum of fedgov "assistance," Texas tried to take care of its own, but the system was overwhelmed.

Tens of thousands of scared, angry, hungry people were camped on the flats outside Austin. Most were decent folks who were down on their luck, but there were plenty of bad apples in the bunch. The people cluster grew explosively, with hundreds more arriving daily. The police tried to fight it at first, but for every vagrant they floated out of the county, ten more sprang up to take his place. The makeshift settlement took on an air of permanency, like all the other shantytowns that were popping up outside the cities.

Trouble came with the squatters. Hard-pressed police were barely able to keep the peace in Austin. They didn't even try to enforce the law in Shantytown. The only law there was the law of the jungle. Five or six murders a day, and ten times that on Saturday night. Every vice and crime imaginable was practiced around the clock. Organized gangs preyed on the squatters, and the weakest were the easiest prey. Some of the decent element banded together for self-protection.

The have-nots hungered for something to believe in, a dream, a cause, a reason why they'd been cast down to the bottom of the social pit. The hucksters were quick to cash in on that need. They were like the snake oil salesmen of the old-time medicine shows, but instead of pitching patent medicine cure-alls to the rubes, they sold hope.

They were preachers, prophets, hate-mongers, apostles of Universal Love, technocrats, machine-breakers, idealists, idiots, and, mostly, rabble rousers. All found a following in Shantytown. Many were already on file in the Bunco Squad's computerized index of confidence tricksters, swindlers, and grifters. The spellbinders turned up the oratorical fire under the cauldron of humanity and set it to boiling.

The flurry of social activism climaxed in the disastrous March on the Capitol. Various factional leaders managed to suppress their mutual detestation long enough to form a coalition for the demonstration. United in protest, their many followers would march from Shantytown to the capitol in

Austin, rallying at the statehouse to present the governor with a petition for a redress of grievances. Anyway, that was the plan.

The governor let it be known that he'd be out of town on that day, but that didn't stop the march. Politicians and state employees also absented themselves well in advance of the deadline.

The situation was a lawman's nightmare. If the horde should run riot in the city, they'd strip it like a flock of locusts. The city police concentrated their forces to protect the downtown business and commercial districts. The corporations and affluent residential enclaves were guarded by their own private police forces. Respectable neighborhoods unable to afford private protection formed their own citizen's militias.

The Rangers were left holding the bag. Like always.

The Texas Rangers were still the state's preemininent law enforcement agency in 2030, continuing a proud two-hundred-year-old tradition of excellence. Operating under the unlikely aegis of the statewide Department of Public Safety, they worked directly for the governor, helping outgunned and undermanned local police and sheriff's departments keep the peace and crack the big cases. Never numbering more than 500 Rangers on its rolls at any one time, the elite body had been attrited down to about 350 members by 2030. They were the best of the best, hard-charging and incorruptible.

They were charged with the duty of protecting the capitol. They were already stretched thin by having all Texas as their bailiwick. They gathered their reserves and tackled the job. The core of their defense was a seventy-five-member Tactical Unit, buttressed by an equal number from other Ranger units. The main force was concentrated at the statehouse. Smaller squads were posted at strategic sites on the grounds, along the line of march, and at the choke points of key routes into the city.

Ranger Command had a bad feeling about the march. Crime intelligence analysts had reported a recent ferment in the underworld—unprecedented alliances between former enemies, large transfers of cash, the stockpiling of weapons, and uneasy truces that quelled gang warfare. Each item was a piece of a puzzle adding up to—what?

As the day of the march dawned, it was obvious that the ranks of the protestors had been swelled by hundreds of the toughest, most violent hoodlums in all Texas. Hitmen, shooters, strong-arm goons, *pistoleros*.

Headquarters knew that the best insurance policy was a big gun, and nothing stopped a mob like an energy weapon. The Rangers had a blaze gun, the existence of which was a tightly guarded secret. Technically it was unauthorized ordnance, a class 3 self-propelled burner mini-cannon. It was smuggled into the statehouse before first light, hidden in the container box of a big-rig suspensor barge freightliner that was supposed to be delivering another load of plastex barricades.

Gangland used the march as a Trojan horse. An army of killers used the genuine demonstrators as a human shield to cover their approach to the capitol. The real target was the Rangers themselves. They'd been a painful thorn in the underworld's hide for too long. Pulling the strings on the crooks from behind the scenes were unknown master plotters, conspiring on behalf of sinister forces whose designs on Texas could never be achieved while the Rangers stood in their way.

The killers were well paid, well armed, and well prepared. They made an effort to blend in, to look as if they belonged among the squatters. They dressed down, walked soft, and kept their hardware under wraps. Generally they were able to carry off the masquerade, as long as nobody looked too closely. Those who did wound up behind the bushes with their throats cut.

By noon, the capitol's South Park was packed with twenty-five thousand people. The Rangers had a pretty good idea of what was brewing. Spy rays scanned hard knots of tough men scattered among the masses. Unease spread throughout the crowd. Sheep grow anxious when wolves are among the fold.

Gunfire sounded from one of the cross streets west of the park. A patrol had discovered heavily armed ground cars massing for a mobile attack. The patrolmen gave a good account of themselves, but they were outgunned a hundred to one. Slugs sieved them and their car was blown up.

Pandemonium engulfed the scene as twenty-five thousand people stampeded in a blind panic. Gang gunmen whipped out their weapons and opened fire. They were armed with machine pistols, sawed-off wheel auto-guns, subguns, carbines. There were some mini-missile launchers, burners, and a few beamer tubes, too. Gun squads popped up throughout the crowd and started blasting at the Rangers guarding the statehouse. If any citizens got in their way, they cut them down, too. And there was no way that the citizens could avoid getting in their way, not in that densely packed mob.

That's when most of the civilians were killed, in the first furious minutes of the fight. Gunmen used the innocent as human shields. The Rangers couldn't effectively return fire without massacring scores of men, women, and children. The killers were under no such restraint.

The Rangers took cover. Sharpshooters with needle-ray burner rifles did their best to thin out the gang gun squads in the front ranks, but otherwise the defenders held their fire.

The innocent dupes had to be dispersed before the Rangers could launch an effective counterattack. They visored down, sealing their helmets, making their light battle suits airtight.

Gas guns were moved to the front, multi-barrel mortars lobbing chem rounds into the plaza. The first salvo loosed clouds of noxious vom gas, inducing instant violent nausea in any who caught so much as a whiff of it.

Next came Blister Fog, a nerve agent irritant whose slightest touch on bare skin caused it to break out in a mass of hives and to itch maddeningly for twenty minutes after exposure. Vom gas took the fight out of rioters and Blister Fog sent them on their way.

That's how it worked on the protesters. Hundreds were trampled in the rush to flee; dozens died underfoot. Many more were killed when they charged blindly into the killer gun squads. Scores succumbed to respiratory failure and acute allergic reactions to the crowd control chemicals. But the vast majority of the marchers cleared out of the plaza fast, leaving the field to those who came to fight and kill.

At the start of the chem shelling, the attackers had donned protective hoods, goggles, and filtered face-hugging gas masks. They wore skintight gloves and tucked their pants into their boots, leaving no bare skin exposed to the Blister Fog.

They nearly stormed the capitol with their first wild rush. Rangers poured gunfire into them, mowing them down until their gun barrels glowed red-hot, breaking the charge.

The attackers took cover and dug in, holding the ground they'd gained.

There was a lull in the action. It lasted long enough for the Rangers to learn they were on their own. Anarchy ruled Austin, it was in full riot. The city cops couldn't come to the rescue, and the private cops wouldn't. The Rangers would just have to save themselves.

Well, it wouldn't be the first time.

The mobile attack came at mid-afternoon. Crimedom had amassed its own armored assault force. They'd rounded up over a dozen heavy-duty vehicles: sixteen-wheeled ground trucks, bulldozers, backhoes, farm tractors, monster trucks, even a midsize suspensor barge. These had been customized into war wagons, armored with thin sheets of metalloy plate, and armed with heavy machine guns, rocket and mini-missile launchers, and recoilless rifles.

A separate force of eight Ninja Jeep FAVs served as a kind of cavalry.

The vehicles rumbled north across the plaza in mass assault. Standing off at a distance, they opened fire. The stately red granite capitol building took a terrible pounding.

The attackers unleashed what they thought was their Sunday punch. An ancient early-model beam projector was mounted on a crude firing platform on the suspensor barge. The floating barge drifted forward of the front line, its driver and four-man gun crew dressed in thick quilted insulation suits and sheltered by plastex sheets. Long narrow slits were cut into the plastex to serve as gun and observation ports.

The beam projector was an antique industrial arc welder that renegade armorers had converted into a beam hurler. The conversion didn't take. When the projector was switched on, it belched streams of sparks for about thirty seconds, then overheated and blew up before the crew could jump to safety. The blast destroyed the barge and crippled the three assault vehicles nearest to it.

The attackers pressed on despite the setback. Fierce fighting followed, with no quarter asked or given by either side. In the end, it was the blaze gun that saved the Rangers from defeat. The class 3 burner mini-cannon's firepower was a whole order greater than anything the attackers possessed. Plus it was the X-factor, the unforeseen variable that the enemy was prepared to counter.

Time and again, a ruby ray of concentrated hellfire speared the crooks' assault vehicles in their most vulnerable spots. The Light That Burns pierced armor plating, turning fuel tanks into firebombs, cremating the carriers and their crews.

When all but a few of the armored attack vehicles had been turned into molten slag heaps, the enemy withdrew from the field, but not from the battle.

They were closer to achieving their goal than they knew. The long day's slaughter had virtually wiped out the defenders. Only thirty-five Rangers remained alive in the statehouse ruins, and only twenty-seven of those were combat effective. One last all-out push would have finished them, but the crooks didn't know that.

The armored attack had failed. Now they would try Juggernaut.

A team of the killers stormed a nearby construction site, to the south, where a massive effort was under way to provide temporary housing for the homeless hordes of Shantytown. They hijacked a Juggernaut Blockbuster wrecking machine, started it up, pointed it toward what was left of the capitol, and headed toward it.

The Rangers could see it coming from a long way off. In the distance, it looked like a building that had detached itself from the cityscape and gone for a walk. Even from afar, they could hear it crashing and crunching its way across the countryside.

They were grouped behind the barricades at the south entrance hall of the statehouse building. The historic old capitol was in ruins. Red granite walls had been rent by bomb blasts; they were bullet-pocked, fire-scorched. Part of the lofty dome had been blown away; the rest looked like a cracked, charred eggshell. Not a single pane of glass remained intact anywhere in the building. Many small fires blazed in the deserted sections; the wings had been demolished.

The structure's south side had seen the heaviest fighting. The triumphal arch fronting the main hall entrance had collapsed. Stone fragments as big as wagons lay heaped in front of the portal, blocking it. It was behind this barricade that the Rangers readied to make their last stand.

The murky air seethed with a witch's brew of smoke, dust, and toxic gases, but the defenders' airtight suits protected them from the poisons. Those who were too badly wounded to handle their weapons had been moved to the far end of the space opposite the barricade. Among them was Captain Randolph "Breck" Breckenridge, the unit commander. He looked dead, but was still breathing.

The walls of the chamber behind him had been hung with paintings depicting Davy Crockett and The Surrender of Santa Anna. They had been destroyed early in the fighting, but the tradition behind them could never die. The last of the Rangers would be true to that tradition. There would be no retreat.

The blaze gun's oversized power-cell storage batteries were almost depleted, with only a few charges left. Even at full power, it would have been unable to stop Juggernaut. The Blockbuster was just too big, a colossal engine of destruction.

"You can't kill that thing with body blows. You've got to go after its head," Smith said.

"What are you waiting for? Let's go, partner," Guthrie said.

Albert Smith, Ranger. Some years earlier, he'd been a military policeman stationed at Space City near Houston, where the rockets went up. He'd been on the graveyard shift the night of August 20, the night that the space base was attacked by a platoon of thirty Avenging Angel death commandos. The Texas-Utah War was already heating up nicely by then, but the Texans had never expected that the enemy would make such a daring strike deep in the heartland. After a red night of slaughter, the invaders were all dead. Smith and two other MPs survived. They were awarded a fistful of medals and the thanks of grateful Texas. Someone pinned the nickname "Alamo" on Smith and it stuck. Eighteen months later he got out of the hospital and joined the Rangers.

It was a hard life and he liked it just fine. He was proud to wear the badge and he was never, ever bored. He'd been in plenty of tight spots and squeezed out of them. He'd cleaned up crime mobs, tamed towns, cracked baffling cases. He'd known fear, too, lots of times, but he'd fought it down and kept on doing what had to be done, and the opposition had always folded first.

Dan Guthrie was the same way. He was big, too, not as tall as Smith but broader in the chest and arms. They were two of a kind, and once they were teamed as partners, they tied into the lawless like twin tornadoes.

Smith had a plan. Juggernaut's "brain" was the human crew operating it from the control cabin. Kill them, and the Blockbuster went brain-dead.

A courier from Headquarters had arrived earlier, flying his sky cycle through the hole in the domed roof and landing on the wide, circular floor of the rotunda. The aircraft was a two-man job, armed with a machine gun in the nose and two side-mounted missiles. Guthrie took the controls. Smith collected four beamer tubes and climbed in the seat behind the pilot.

Guthrie started the engine, the rotor noise booming in the vast, echoing chamber. The machine quivered, straining at the leash of gravity. The runners left the floor as it lifted.

The round floor shrank and the hole in the roof grew as the sky cycle ascended. It flitted through the hole and outside, into the sunset sky.

The plaza below was a killing field carpeted with the bodies of machines and human dead. It was cratered, scorched, and scarred—black smoke, red flames, gray sky.

The sky cycle swooped south, a metal dragonfly. Patches of smoke and toxic gas quilted the grounds. At the opposite end of the plaza, Juggernaut marched inexorably onward.

Construction requires destruction. Clearing precedes building. Juggernaut was a wholesale demolition machine, a Blockbuster urban clearance vehicle. It could wreck a city block at a time, razing the structures, ripping them apart, and grinding them into powder.

It was an oblong slab, 40 feet tall, 50 feet wide, and 150 feet long. It was divided lengthwise into ringed segments, each 15-foot segment riding on two sets of treaded tires. It looked like a giant gray caterpillar munching its way across the landscape.

Its front end was fearsome to behold. Its main feature was a rotary cutter head thirty-five-feet in diameter, designed to chew through buildings. The fanlike blades were idling now, but when engaged they would gobble up ferrocrete walls like candy and use metalloy beams for toothpicks. Pulped rubble would be sucked into the huge maw and passed through the machine on conveyor belts while being crushed ever finer by a series of rollers, before being excreted out the stern vents as fine powder.

Gun squads now rode upon the Blockbuster's back like fleas, sheltering behind five rings of heaped sandbags and building blocks. They didn't expect to be attacked from above.

The remnants of the hoodlum army scattered on the ground were taken by surprise by the sudden appearance of the sky cycle. It had covered a good part of the distance to Juggernaut before the gun squads started shooting. The barrage increased as the gap narrowed. The closer the sky cycle came, the thicker the gunfire.

Guthrie flew a frantic evasive pattern, bobbing and weaving, dodging the blasts. No less frantic were the gun squads atop the machine as they wrestled with their weapons, trying to bring them to bear on the onrushing aircraft.

Guthrie dipped low, flying below the top of the Juggernaut, out of the line of fire from the gun crews. The sky cycle's speed made the Blockbuster seem to rush past like a speeding express train.

Slugs and shrapnel peppered the air. The sky cycle zipped past Juggernaut's tail, swung around in a rising curve, and came up behind it.

The aircraft flew up the length of the Blockbuster, making a strafing run that caught the gun crews flat-footed. They were still trying to swivel their heavy tripod-mounted guns to the rear to meet the threat when the sky cycle's machine gun opened up.

.50-caliber rounds ripped through the crew gunners, raining down from above, ventilating them. They screamed, spun, then sprawled dead and dying, their blood soaking the shredded sandbags.

As the aircraft neared the head of the machine, a line of liquid light spurted past, blurring the air with heat waves. Guthrie and Smith could feel the heat through their suits.

A crook in the forward gun nest nearest the cutting face was wielding a plasmatic blowtorch. He whipped it through the air like a garden hose, trying to tag the sky cycle.

He came close, so close that the super-heated air of its passage buffeted the aircraft. Guthrie banked hard left while Smith fired a beamer tube.

The bolt of manmade lightning missed the target but struck close enough to the gun crew to hurt them. The blast cratered the hull plate, knocking the crew off their feet, breaking up their timing.

The sky cycle swung around again, this time attacking from the front, rushing toward a head-on collision with the cutting face. It popped up at the last second, almost level with the gun crew.

Smith fired another beamer tube, electrocuting the gunners. The torch wielder bounced out of the nest as if he were on a trampoline, crashing to his back ten paces away.

"Take her as low as you can go and hold her! I'm going in," Smith said.

As Juggernaut's front crossed the halfway mark to the statehouse, the sky cycle came under the heaviest firing yet. On the west side of the plaza, a low retaining wall thrust into the pavilion to contain a modest-sized monument on a triangular piece of ground. Bordering the wedge-shaped space, the wall jogged around it, then resumed its regular course, edging the plaza. The monument featured a statue on a pedestal and stone columns and benches, providing much cover. Early in the battle, a gun squad had occupied the space inside this deadly angle, a strong point from which they had taken a heavy toll of Rangers while suffering minimal losses themselves.

Realizing the threat from the Rangers on the sky cycle, the gunmen from the deadly angle turned their firepower on it just as Smith went over the side, dropping down on Juggernaut.

"Give me some covering fire to pin those guys down, Dan!"

"Will do. Give 'em hell, Al!"

A fusillade from the deadly angle tore across the top of Juggernaut's head, ripping Smith and the sky cycle's undercarriage.

Body armor absorbed the blows, but the impact knocked Smith down and rolling. Clawing at the hull plate, he managed to stop short of tumbling off the starboard edge. He'd had to let go of the two beamer tube launchers he'd taken with him. One went over the side; the other was stopped by his own body.

Guthrie pulled back hard on the stick, causing the sky cycle to zoom straight up for a hundred feet. The aircraft shuddered from the rough handling, but so far it had sustained only minor damage.

Slugs sleeted through the air as the gun squad tried to knock down the sky cycle. Its nose dipped, lining the machine gun up with the deadly angle, but before Guthrie could fire, something whooshed past his head, scaring the hell out of him.

It was a mini-missile, and it had only missed him by a hair, shooting through the space between the underside of the rotor cage and the top of the fuselage. A stringlike vapor trail led back to its point of origin, a launcher being operated by an enemy missileer on the roof of a building behind the deadly angle.

The missileer was not alone. Others like him were scattered across the roof, swinging their multi-tube launchers toward Guthrie. He nosed up the sky cycle to level the machine gun on them, only to be hit from below.

The sky cycle rocked from the impact of slugs tearing through the nose. Shrapnel hit Guthrie's face-plate and chest, causing him to throw up his hands. That saved him, because letting go of the controls caused the sky cycle to veer wildly to one side, spoiling the aim of both missileers and gunmen.

The aircraft slewed sideways and down until Guthrie grabbed the controls and stabilized it. He was lucky. He hadn't been hurt, just startled. The sky cycle was still fully operational.

Duty demanded that he swing around and make another run against the foe, trying to finish them off in a kill-or-be-killed showdown. But he just didn't have the stomach for it. He'd come out of that last engagement by the skin of his teeth and had no desire to charge down the barrels of the missileers and the gun squad. There was no sense in pushing his luck too far.

Besides, no matter what the outcome of the battle, the Rangers were finished. Today's slaughter had dealt a death blow to the outfit. The gun gangs would never have dared their attack without the covert support of some very big people, ruthless power brokers who had determined that the Texas Rangers must die. Guthrie had sense enough to see which way the wind was blowing. He'd have to be some kind of damned fool to throw his life away on a lost cause.

Even before his train of thought had reached its conclusion, he'd already made his decision. Instead of returning to the fray, he pointed the sky cycle at an open space in the wall of buildings hemming the plaza. Beyond that space lay escape, safety, life itself.

"Dan! Dan! Where are you going?!"

Smith's voice, disbelieving, calling him over the comm link.

"Dan, wait! *Dan*—"

Guthrie switched off the in-helmet radio, silencing Smith's desperate outcries.

"Sorry, amigo, but I've got to look out for Number One," he said, talking to himself, since he had closed down communication with his brother Ranger.

Just to make it look good, Guthrie jiggled the stick around a little, rocking the sky cycle to make it appear that it was out of control. Flashing through the gap, he broke out of the battle zone into the blessed open and kept on going.

Smith lay flattened on Juggernaut. His helmet's extro audio mikes picked up the sound of the gun squad cheering and laughing at having made the sky cycle turn tail and run.

Five gun nests were in place atop the 150-foot length of the giant machine. Most of the gun crews had been killed in the strafing runs, but a few were only wounded. They started shooting at Smith with handguns and rifles, the bullets whipping over his head.

He fired his last beamer tube at them, unleashing a sizzling bolt of man-made lightning that skimmed along Juggernaut's spine, cutting the feet out from under his assailants. They fired no more.

The weapons in the forward gun nest were damaged beyond use, but perhaps not in the next one down the line. As Smith crawled toward it, he passed the plasmatic torch wielder's corpse. The tool seemed unharmed, functional.

The missileers on the rooftop had ignored him to concentrate on the sky cycle, but no longer. They hesitated to fire, perhaps for fear of damaging Juggernaut. But no mere barrage of mini-missiles could derail the Blockbuster, although they could finish off Smith, as the missileers were sure to realize in a matter of seconds.

Smith rose, rushing the gun nest, diving into it headfirst. Praying that the tripod-mounted heavy machine gun still worked, he swung up the barrel toward the rooftop and pulled the trigger.

The weapon chattered, spewing a stream of slugs. Smith found the range and swept it across the rooftop's edge, chopping the missileers who had gathered there.

They were done for, but so was the ammunition. Abandoning the gun nest, he started back toward the head of the machine. Heavy fire from the deadly angle sought to stop him.

Stretched out beside the torch wielder, Smith tore the nozzle gun from his dead hand. The torch was an Infernex model, a medium-sized piece of equipment compared to the top-of-the-line Holocauster, but it still packed plenty of punch. Gauges on the container backpack showed that the gas tanks were still over half-full.

Smith's light battle armor was fast reaching the breaking point from the terrible battering inflicted by the deadly angle guns. The slugs flattened and failed to penetrate, but each hit carried a terrific wallop. The cuirass was fast approaching the point when it would come apart from the stress. The plasmatic torch was built tough, especially the container, but if a slug cut the tube to the nozzle gun, he'd be out of business—out of life.

The statehouse's shattered southern face loomed up, blocking out more of the landscape as Juggernaut neared its goal.

Smith pointed the nozzle gun at the deadly angle and squeezed the trigger. The plasmatic stream spurted out with a hissing roar like the gates of Hell being opened.

All gunfire from the deadly angle ceased.

Juggernaut's operating cab was in the front of the machine. A crude but effective housing of metalloy plates had been welded over the windshield, grille, and sides of the cab to shield the operators. They were driving blind, steering the Blockbuster by inboard directional finders.

Smith took the backpack container harness off the dead man, and crawled to Juggernaut's front edge. The nozzle gun was in one hand while the other dragged the container behind him.

Pointing the nozzle down at the slanted metalloy plate covering the windshield, he sprayed it with the plasma stream.

Even through his insulated armor, the heat was terrific. He felt as if he were being boiled alive in his battle suit. Darkness pressed in on him as he fought to keep from blacking out.

The metalloy shielding plate reddened. It was yellow where the plasma hit it, and white-hot in the center of the blast area. The plate softened, rippling at first, then running like hot wax.

It couldn't have been too pleasant in the operator's cabin. If the crewmen screamed, Smith didn't hear them over the streaming plasma.

The white-hot center dimpled, then collapsed, spewing molten metalloy into the cab. Smith poured the super-heated liquid light through the hole in the plate, filling the control room with sun fire.

The plate sagged in the middle and then collapsed completely. The operator's cab was a boxful of hell. Smith kept pumping it full of plasma.

Juggernaut lurched, groaned, and shuddered to a stop in the middle of the capitol steps.

Easing his finger off the trigger, Smith shut off the plasma stream before passing out.

TWELVE

Now:

" . . . LATER, I HEARD that Smith was dead, killed in action," Guthrie said.

"Apparently you were misinformed."

"Don't try me, Breedlove."

"Sorry, sir. But what does it all mean?"

"Did you ever hear the story about the Last Rangers?"

"The . . . Last Rangers? I believe I have heard the term, in passing, not that I paid much attention to it. I don't put much stock in popular superstition, the myths that the rabble create to give themselves something to believe in."

"Maybe you better wipe that smug smile off your face and think again."

"You're not seriously suggesting that Smith's ghost has come back from the dead to, er, fight crime and injustice, are you, sir?"

"I said, don't try me, Breedlove. It wasn't a ghost at Beamer Junction. A spook didn't shoot up Molehill and steal a cybernetic brain out of that APU."

"I agree with you there, sir."

Guthrie stroked his chin. His eyes had a faraway look.

"Those college professors of yours must have told you that every legend has a basis in fact, Breedlove. Those Last Ranger stories first started shortly after the real Rangers were wiped out in the sneak rocket attack on Ranger Headquarters a few months after the Battle of the Capitol Steps."

"An obvious compensatory mechanism in the collective psyche of the common folk. Unable to face reality, they take refuge in a myth about a band of ghostly champions who live in a hole in the earth, biding their time until a distant day of judgment when they will emerge with an arsenal of super-weapons to rescue the good and destroy evildoers. Which is the legend of the Last Rangers in a nutshell. Similar myth cycles are associated with Frederick Barbarossa and King Arthur, among others. It's a universal folkloric motif."

Guthrie stood up, jammed his hands in his pockets, and began pacing the narrow confines of the dome.

"But what if it's not a myth, Breedlove? What if it's just a scrambled version of the truth? Ranger Command was smart as hell. They could have seen the handwriting on the wall and taken steps to prepare for it. Suppose they set up a secret headquarters, in a cave, maybe—that would tie in with the part of the legend about the Last Rangers living in a hole in the earth. Say they only pretended to be wiped out, to throw the enemies off the trail while they go underground and build up their strength for a comeback."

"I'd say that's a lot of supposing, sir."

"And what about that cybernetic brain? Those old APUs had some damned advanced hardware in them, stuff that they've forgotten how to duplicate today."

"That is true. I've heard it said that liquid crystal colloid computers were the closest thing to artificial intelligence ever developed," Breedlove said.

For the first time in the conversation he seemed thoughtful, as if he was starting to seriously consider the possibilities.

Guthrie slammed a fist into his palm. "There! You see, that proves what I said. Smith's got a reason for grabbing that cybernetic super-brain, by God!"

"An artificially intelligent computer would have a multiplicity of uses. It could control a squadron of warplanes, tap into the glo-beam information net, take over lesser computer networks, manipulate ultra-sophisticated weapon systems, possibly even design whole new classes of E-weps . . ."

"Now you're talking like a believer," Guthrie said, grinning.

"It's a wild theory, but if there's even a chance that it's true, Commissioner Piper must be told about it immediately!"

"That's where we're going, sonny—pronto!"

As Gottschalk's men removed the camo cloaking tarps from the Raptor, Guthrie handed the pilot a note.

"Couple of changes in our flight path, Tim," he said.

"Whatever you say, Mr. Guthrie," the pilot said, after reading the note.

Pitiless sunlight blazed off the reflective surfaces of the plane, making it look molten. Tim, Guthrie, and Breedlove climbed into the cockpit.

After a routine preflight check, Tim started the engines. The comm shack reported no traces of enemy EMG surveillance, a finding which was confirmed by the Raptor's detectors. All was cleared for takeoff.

Turbines howled as the aircraft began its vertical ascent, the afterburners kicking up a dust storm in the pocket canyon.

When the Raptor had risen above the canyon walls, into the open, it took off in a straight line, vectoring at high velocity.

It flew northwest, into the desert, rather than northeast to Santone.

Breedlove fidgeted. After fifteen minutes of direct flight deep into the heart of the desert wilderness, he could contain himself no longer.

"This is a roundabout way home," he said.

"Claggard's put his air patrols on full alert ever since that business at Molehill. We're detouring to avoid his detectors," Guthrie said.

Hurtling along at near supersonic speeds, the Raptor crossed into the Badlands. Spidery cracks that were deep chasms were strung like webs across the blistering sandy wastes.

"This is far enough, Tim."

"Roger, Mr. Guthrie."

Breedlove glanced at Guthrie, who was grinning with a mouthful of crocodile teeth, and in that instant, he *knew*.

"Bye bye," Guthrie said.

Tim hit the ejector seat button. Breedlove's chair catapulted out of the pop-top escape hatch, taking Breedlove with it. He was shot out of the plane and into empty air.

After a pause, the chair's chutes opened and it drifted slowly down to earth, the only sign of movement as far as the eye could see on that broiling landscape.

"He's so smart, let's see him think his way out of that hell."

"I never liked the guy myself, Mr. Guthrie."

"Let's head for home, Tim."

The plane wheeled around in a great curving turn until it was pointing east, toward distant, mighty Santone.

Guthrie settled back in his seat. Two can keep a secret if one is dead. Breedlove was as good as dead. Nobody could walk sixty miles out of that desert furnace.

Knowledge is power. What he knew and had guessed about Smith was a valuable commodity, one that he planned to milk for all it was worth. He wasn't going to let Breedlove blab it to Piper for free.

Guthrie was busy figuring the best way to parlay his inside information into personal gain when the pilot suddenly gave a start.

"What is it, Tim?"

"I don't know, Mr. Guthrie. Something's screwy here . . ."

Tim flipped switches and turned dials on the instrument panel, anxiously watching the detector readings.

"Weird! First the detector registers an unidentified aerial object, then just as soon as it starts tracking it, it drops off the board," he said.

A shadow fell over Guthrie. Not the shadow of fear, though he felt that, too, but a real shadow. He knew it was real because it fell across Tim, too, darkening the cockpit and making them both look up at the same time.

Through the tinted bubble-top canopy, a torpedo-shaped aircraft could be seen overflying the Raptor, effortlessly pacing it.

Tim swore. Guthrie clawed the arms of his chair as if they were the sanity he was so desperately trying to cling to.

"Hi, Dan."

"Smith!"

Guthrie didn't even wonder how Smith was able to speak to him through the plane's transceiver. It was just one more example of the advanced technology whose mastery of the EMG spectrum had already been amply demonstrated.

"You should have died back there at the capitol, Dan. A lot of good people would be alive today if you had."

"Now, wait a minute, Al—"

"Can't. No time. I'm too busy tying up loose ends, and you're one of them. Remember the Alamo, Dan."

"Don't—!!"

Rockets tore loose from the underside of the cruiser, slanting downward toward the Raptor. When they stabbed into the plane, a fireball blossomed that filled the sky.

Flaming fragments of wreckage were scattered for miles.

In the cruiser cockpit, Alamo Smith flipped the debris a mocking two-finger salute.

"Adios, amigo," he said.

"NICE SHOOTING, RANGER," Bird Dog said.

"Thanks, partner."

Twenty-three thousand miles straight up, the *Lone Star Satellite* maintained its lonely vigil, a sentinel on the edge of cosmic space. Down below, there was trouble . . . like always. But this time, something new had been added:

Hope.